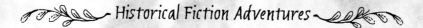
The Locket
Surviving the Triangle Shirtwaist Fire

Suzanne Lieurance

Enslow Publishers, Inc.
40 Industrial Road
Box 398
Berkeley Heights, NJ 07922
USA

http://www.enslow.com

This book is dedicated to my husband, Adrian Lieurance, for his constant help and support, to my editors at Enslow for all their hard work and attention to detail, and to my good friend Jenine Whittecar who helped me bring the characters in this story to life.

Copyright © 2008 by Suzanne Lieurance

All rights reserved.

No part of this book may be reproduced by any means
without the written permission of the publisher.

Library of Congress Cataloging-in-Publication Data:

Lieurance, Suzanne.
    The locket : surviving the Triangle Shirtwaist fire / Suzanne Lieurance.
       p. cm. — (Historical fiction adventures (HFA))
    Summary: After Galena, an eleven-year-old Russian immigrant, survives a terrible fire at the non-unionized Triangle Shirtwaist factory while her older sister and many others do not, she begins fighting for improved working conditions in New York City factories.
    ISBN-13: 978-0-7660-2928-6
    ISBN-10: 0-7660-2928-X
    1. Triangle Shirtwaist Company—Fire, 1911—Juvenile fiction. [1. Triangle Shirtwaist Company—Fire, 1911—Fiction. 2. Sisters—Fiction. 3. Labor unions—Fiction. 4. Immigrants—Fiction. 5. Jews—United States—Fiction. 6. New York (N.Y.)—History—1898–1951—Fiction.] I. Title.
    PZ7.L6194Lo 2008
    [Fic]—dc22   2007005281

Printed in the United States of America

10 9 8 7 6 5 4 3 2 1

To Our Readers: We have done our best to make sure all Internet Addresses in this book were active and appropriate when we went to press. However, the author and the publisher have no control over and assume no liability for the material available on those Internet sites or on other Web sites they may link to. Any comments or suggestions can be sent by e-mail to comments@enslow.com or to the address on the back cover.

Enslow Publishers, Inc. is committed to printing our books on recycled paper. The paper in every book contains between 10% to 30% post-consumer waste (PCW). The cover board on the outside of each book contains 100% PCW. Our goal is to do our part to help young people and the environment too!

Illustration Credits: Library of Congress, pp. 152, 154, 156, 157; © Norma Cornes, Shutterstock.com, pp. 5, 19, 37, 49, 73, 82, 88, 100, 113, 126, 146; Original Painting by © Corey Wolfe, p. 1.

Locket Used on Running Heads: © Joan Loitz, Shutterstock.com.

Cover Illustration: Original Painting by © Corey Wolfe.

Contents

chapter one

My Little Family in This Big City

I t was an early spring morning in New York City but already the day promised to be warm and sunny. I gazed out the window of our tiny apartment on Orchard Street.

Sunlight was straining to poke its way between our towering tenement and the one next to it. But the two buildings were so close and so tall, it was impossible for me to get a decent glimpse of the sky.

Oh, well. It doesn't matter. I'll be outside soon.

Mama and my older sister, Anya, were arguing again. Their angry words gave a chill to our apartment, and I shivered as I pulled my dress on over my head and smoothed it down to get ready for the workday.

I tied back my curly dark brown hair with a green ribbon that matched my dress, then checked my appearance in the small mirror hanging over the creamy white ceramic washbowl and pitcher set resting on the washstand.

I'll never be as beautiful as Anya, I thought as I looked at myself.

Still, with my dark eyes and lashes, full lips, and straight nose, I knew some people thought I was pretty. And that was good enough. I smiled at my reflection, then moved away from the mirror.

A curtain separated our sleeping area from the rest of the single room that made up our apartment. On the other side of the curtain, Anya was trying to make a point with Mama. But it was impossible to have a private conversation in a room that would have been crowded for one person, much less a family of four like ours. The walls were so thin, and so many families were crowded into one building, that it was not unusual for us to hear the neighbors arguing or talking loudly in our Lower East Side tenement.

Yet, although our apartment was only one room, Mama tried to make our home as cozy and as cheerful as she could. Framed photographs of family members left behind in Russia were displayed atop pretty crocheted lace doilies that decorated a pine dresser next to the door to the outside hallway. The smallest photograph of the group was actually the one Mama treasured the most. It was a photo

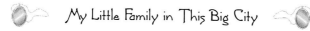
of her older sister, Tatiana, who had died when she was a teenager and Mama was just a child.

Our sleeping area consisted of two feather mattresses (one for Anya and me to share and one for Mama and Papa) on wooden frames, along with the washstand and a line of pegs on the wall for our clothes.

I pulled open the curtain just as a teakettle whistled on the old cast-iron stove where Mama stood.

"But, Mama," protested Anya. "Dmitri thinks . . . "

"Hush now, Anya. I don't care what Dmitri thinks," Mama said in Yiddish. She lifted the kettle from the stove and poured hot water onto a pile of crumbled tea leaves nestled inside an old chipped teapot. "He should stop filling your head with foolish notions."

Anya sat at a small wooden table in a corner of the room across from the stove. A large white sink on the wall completed our small kitchen and living area. Anya answered in English. "But, Mama, they are not foolish notions. Dmitri says the working conditions and pay are much better for those who belong to the garment workers' union. Did you know that if the Triangle factory hired union workers, as Dmitri's does, I would only have to work half a day on Saturdays?"

"It pains me that you have to work on the Sabbath," Mama said. She cut a thick slice of heavy brown bread and handed it to Anya. "But we need the money, and a half

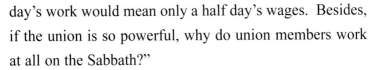

day's work would mean only a half day's wages. Besides, if the union is so powerful, why do union members work at all on the Sabbath?"

I walked over to the wooden cabinet along the wall of the kitchen area and reached up to remove two teacups as I listened to Mama's protests.

No wonder Mama's English is so poor. It will never improve if she refuses to use it.

From the time our family had immigrated to New York City from Russia over a year ago, Anya and I both had been trying very hard to become "real" Americans, even though it would be a while before we could apply for actual citizenship. We spoke only English now and Anya (who was almost eighteen) wore American clothes. Mama said I was too young for the cotton shirtwaists that were currently so popular among Anya and other young women in New York City.

Every day, Anya wore her thick blonde hair piled on her head in the sophisticated Gibson girl hairstyle that was all the rage. Anya was even thinking of changing her name to Anna, so it would sound more American. Unless she spoke, revealing her heavily accented English, no one could tell that she had been in America for just a short part of her life. I knew Anya was proud of that. It had been no fun for either of us as newly arrived immigrants. We were called greenhorns because we did not yet know the

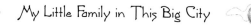

customs and habits of our new country and we were constantly making mistakes. We hated being compared to young animals, like deer or elk, with immature antlers called greenhorns.

Mama resisted the American customs, although Papa often reminded her that the reason we came to this country in the first place was to find a better, different way of life. When we encouraged Mama to try something new that was considered American, she shook her head and told us she was too used to her old Russian ways.

Mama was tall and slender, but she did not seem to care about her appearance. Besides, as a strict religious Jewish woman, she would never change the way she dressed. She wore the same long, drab dresses she had worn in Russia, and she pulled back her beautiful long dark hair and twisted it into a knot at the nape of her neck. She most always wore an apron over her dress and sometimes a scarf on her head, which she tied in the back beneath her hair, making her look serious and stern. I loved to admire her in the evenings, just before she slipped into bed beside Papa. Her hair was down then, and it draped softly over her shoulders. Her simple nightdress with small pink flowers printed on the fabric revealed Mama's gentle, feminine side, which she tried so hard to hide during the day for fear others would think she was weak and attempt to take advantage of her.

As for Papa, he was a quiet man who seldom contradicted Mama. He woke each morning before daylight, went to work, and came home exhausted every night. Yet, tired as he always was, occasionally he brought home the pieces of several garments and stitched them together to make a bit of extra money. Usually, however, he only managed to eat a few bites of supper before falling into bed. Mama, Anya, and I tried not to disturb his sleep as we washed the supper dishes, quietly discussing the day's events until we got ready for bed ourselves each evening.

"No, Mama," answered Anya now. "Better wages *and* only a half day's work on Saturday."

Mama threw her arms into the air. "Hmph. . . . It is still a foolish notion to think they will pay you more for less work, I tell you."

I sat down beside Anya and looked at her. "I think Mama is right, Anya. Dmitri is a man. Maybe the union is right for him, but that does not mean it is right for you. It might be dangerous for a young woman."

Mama handed me a slice of the dark, dense bread and poured tea into the cup in front of me.

"Can't you just be happy that you have a job?" I asked Anya. "I am. It's only because we all have jobs that we don't have to take in boarders as so many other families here must do."

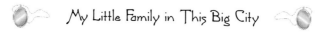

I knew Mama was particularly proud that only our immediate family lived in our tiny apartment. So many other families were forced to take in boarders, people who paid them to share their home and meals.

I was proud of myself, too, because at just eleven years old, I was helping support my family. At first, Mama had wanted me to go to school, as I had done in Russia. But there were simply too many living expenses here in this new country. We needed my wages, and I was happy to work, even though I wasn't legally of age to do so. This is one reason I was against the union. If shops hired only union workers I would not be allowed to work until I was old enough to join the union. To me, working was very important. It meant I was not just a child any longer. I was one of the millions of working girls in America. I liked that. I was proud to help out, and I did not want that pride to be taken away from me if Anya joined the union and made more money so my wages would not be needed.

Anya's face softened as she looked over at me. "Of course, I am happy that I have a job, Little Shadow," she said.

I smiled at the use of the pet name she had given me when I was small and followed her everywhere she went.

"But Dmitri says working conditions could be much better for everyone if we all belonged to the union," continued Anya. "And that's why I want to attend one of the union meetings. To see what it is all about."

Mama joined us at the table. "No more talk of Dmitri and unions," she said as she sat down. "One of the reasons we left Russia was because it was not safe for us there. When I was a child, there was always trouble whenever people gathered in large groups. There were many beatings and often people died . . ." Her words trailed off and she seemed lost in thought. I knew she was thinking about her own sister, Tatiana, who had been killed during the pogroms—organized riots directed at the Jews—that swept through Russia when Tatiana was a teenager and Mama was just six. Back then, most Jews lived in provinces of Russia called the Pale and were forbidden to live in the gentile, or non-Jewish, provinces. Mama's family lived in the shadows of their small village and tried to be as unnoticeable as possible. "Bad things always seemed to happen to people who attracted attention," Mama had once told me.

On a quiet afternoon so long ago, Mama and her sister had been sent on a simple errand. They were supposed to come right home when they had finished it. Their mother had no way of knowing that soldiers were on their way to the village to cause trouble for any Jews they happened to come across. The government tried to convince everyone that Jews had been responsible for the murder of the Czar

Alexander II and his family, although there was no evidence to support this claim, and they terrorized the Jewish villages from time to time.

Mama loved to hide from Tatiana as a kind of game. That day, she hid behind bales of hay in the blacksmith's barn just before the soldiers arrived and the violence outside on the streets started. Tatiana shouted for Mama. Then, knowing she could not run home without her sister, she went looking for her.

Mama told me the last words she heard Tatiana call out to her were, "Come, Little Sister, we must hurry home. Do not hide from me."

But Mama had not known what her sister was talking about because she had not heard the riot erupting outside in the streets. Mama stayed in her hiding place, quietly giggling as she waited for her sister to find her.

Tatiana had just walked into the barn to look for Mama when two angry young men dressed in uniforms grabbed her from behind and pinned her to the ground. Mama was paralyzed with fear as she peeked around the bales of hay and saw the men attacking her sister. The men forced kisses on Tatiana and pulled at her clothes.

Mama was horrified at what she saw, but she knew she could not help her sister. She could only close her eyes so she would not have to witness the cruelty to Tatiana and stay silent and hidden behind the hay so the men would not know she was there. Otherwise, they would harm her, too.

Finally, when the men had left the barn, Mama opened her eyes again.

Tatiana lay dead in the hay. Outside on the streets, other innocent Jews lay injured or dead, too.

Once all of the soldiers had ridden away, and the crowds of villagers had returned to their homes, Mama raced home and led her parents back to the gruesome spot where her sister had been killed. And now, all these years later, Mama still could not seem to forget the constant danger and violence of her childhood. She had also never forgiven herself for hiding in the blacksmith's barn that afternoon, giving those two awful men the opportunity to attack and kill her innocent sister. This guilt made Mama determined that Anya and I would live safe and peaceful lives. That meant we should never go anywhere, even to a union meeting, without Mama's approval. I thought Mama's fears were unfounded, and I had told her so once. I still remember what she said. "Your life experiences make you who you are forever, Galena. Crowds always make me fearful. I don't know that I'll ever get over that."

Suddenly Mama looked back at Anya. "Didn't Dmitri tell you about the Uprising of the 20,000 a few years ago? It was a dangerous strike. Some of the picketers were beaten or put in jail. I will not have that happen to my girl, my *shaineh meydls*."

Mama always called Anya and me her shaineh meydls, which was Yiddish for "beautiful girls." Now Mama took Anya's face in her hands and looked Anya straight in the eye. "And don't be so friendly with Dmitri, my child. The *shadchen* has found a possible match for you. Next week you will meet the man who just may be your perfect husband. Now . . . finish your breakfast or you will be late for work."

I took a few sips of the hot tea and ate my bread. I did not realize that Mama had enough money for a shadchen, a professional matchmaker. Mama must have been putting aside a few coins for months in order to pay a shadchen. This was serious.

Mama must be more upset than I am that Anya has been spending so much time with Dmitri if she is paying a matchmaker.

Anya did not look very happy at Mama's mention of the shadchen, but she knew better than to complain to Mama about it. It would only start another argument, and we did not have time for that right now. We were already in danger of being late for work. We could not let that happen. It would mean our pay would be docked, or, worse yet, we could be fired. Then what would we do?

Anya got up from the table and grabbed her pocketbook from the dresser.

I brushed crumbs from the table and stood up, too. Mama handed Anya a large lump of newsprint that contained the bread and cheese she and I would eat later for lunch. We kissed Mama on both cheeks and lifted our scarves and coats from the pegs by the front door.

Mama would work today, too, although she did not have to leave our home. Every morning after Anya and I left the apartment, neighbor women arrived at our door and joined Mama at our kitchen table, assembling artificial flowers all day that would be sewed onto ladies' hats. At first, it was strange to see Mama putting artificial flowers together. Back in Russia, we lived on a small parcel of land where Mama raised chickens for their eggs. We also had a cow that provided us with milk and butter. Taking care of the animals and tending to the vegetables Mama grew in the warmer months of the year was important work. Much more important than making flowers for ladies' hats.

But in so many ways our lives here were much different from what they had been in Russia. Mama did less important work now, and Papa said we must try to "blend in" with everyone else. For Papa, that meant cutting his hair and trimming his beard, something that would have been an outright sin back home in Russia. At first it had been a shock to see Papa change his appearance

so drastically. But he assured us that God realized he was still the same kind and gentle man at heart and would not punish him for conforming to life in this new place.

Blend in . . . yes, that's exactly what Anya and I are trying to do, and we are still the same kind girls at heart, too.

"Come, Galena," said Anya. "Dmitri will be on the street waiting for us."

Anya opened the door to the outside hallway. At once I smelled coffee, cooked fish, and stale cabbage that wafted through the air—smells left over from a neighbor's supper last night. We navigated our way down the stairs among young men and women who were also headed to work. We passed dirty children playing in the dark stairwells. I heard babies crying behind closed doors.

At the bottom of the stairs, I pulled on Anya's sleeve. "May I see the locket now, please?" I asked Anya.

Anya's most prized possession was her beautiful gold locket. It always hung from a chain around her neck, although she tucked it inside her clothes on workdays, so it would not get tangled in the sewing machines and choke her. Our grandmother, or Bubbie as we called her in Yiddish, had given the locket to Anya before we left Russia, and Anya had promised her she would never take it off. Inside the locket were two faded, but treasured, photographs—one of Mama, Papa, Anya, and me, and one

17

of our beloved Bubbie. Every morning when we left the apartment, I asked to open the locket and admire the photos. It made me feel closer to Mama and Papa when I knew I would not be seeing them all day. And it always made me feel closer to Bubbie since I knew we would probably never see her again. She had been too old and feeble to make the trip to America with us, so she had stayed in Russia with Mama's younger sister and her husband.

Anya knew how it comforted me to see those family photos, so she was always willing to let me open the locket and admire them for a few moments.

Anya pulled the locket from the neckline of her blouse and opened the locket so I could peek inside at the photos.

I smiled at the photos and blew them a kiss. "Good morning, sweet Bubbie. Good-bye, Mama and Papa. I will miss you today while I am at work."

Anya smiled at the photos, too, then snapped the locket shut and stuffed it back inside her blouse.

chapter two

Working Through the Day

I pushed open the door to the sidewalk and we stepped outside. On the front stoop a young boy was yelling, "Paper! Get your morning paper!" as he held up a newspaper so everyone could see the day's headlines.

Dmitri was there, too, studying the sidewalk as he paced in front of the building. He wore a soft brown cap. Dark curls stuck out underneath it.

"Dmitri," shouted Anya.

Dmitri looked up and noticed us approaching him. He was waiting for us, as he did every morning. His dark eyes sparkled when he spotted Anya, and he smiled, revealing gleaming white teeth, straight as a measuring stick.

"Ah, there you are," said Dmitri. "Good morning, ladies. We must not be late for work. Let us walk quickly."

Like both of us, Dmitri was a garment worker. But he did not work at the same factory as Anya and I. Several months ago, Anya was introduced to Dmitri by a friend of hers named Leah who worked with Dmitri. Dmitri had convinced Leah to join the union, and now she was even more into it than Dmitri.

Almost as soon as he met Anya, Dmitri started trying to convince her to support the struggle for better working conditions by joining the Garment Workers' Union. Each morning he accompanied us to the Asch building, where Anya and I both labored at the Triangle Shirtwaist Company, located on the eighth, ninth, and tenth floors. After he dropped us off, he hurried to his job, which was a few blocks away. Every afternoon, he returned to the Asch building to walk us home. He said it was not safe for two "gentle ladies" like Anya and me to be walking the city streets alone.

"He's just trying to flatter us, Anya," I had told her. "Everyone walks the streets of the city during the day. We don't need for him to be our bodyguard. He's too bossy. He just wants you to join the union. That's why he's so friendly toward you."

Anya had laughed and said, "I think it's sweet that he wants to protect us."

But today I frowned at his usual domineering ways. He was irritating. But besides that, if I were honest with myself, I had to admit I was more than a little jealous of Dmitri, too. Since Anya had met him, she had less and less time for me, and now the two of them were always laughing and whispering together, like they had some strange secret that Anya refused to share. Before Dmitri came along, Anya had shared everything with me, and I knew I was her best friend as well as her sister. Now things were different.

Why did Dmitri have to enter our lives and come between my sister and me? Leah might be Anya's friend, but she is certainly no friend of mine after introducing her to this pushy man!

I was trying to think of something more pleasant than Leah or Dmitri when Leah herself appeared at the end of our street and stood at the corner waiting for us.

"Oh, look!" said Anya, waving at her. "There's Leah. She can walk to work with us."

"Good morning, Leah," said Anya as we joined her at the corner. "How nice to meet like this."

My bad mood must have been evident from the look on my face because after Leah said hello to Anya and Dmitri, she touched my shoulder and asked, "What's the matter, Galena? Aren't you feeling well today?"

Leah was a plain girl with a large nose and a shrill voice.

Even a shadchen would have trouble finding a match for this girl, I thought to myself as I tried to smile at her.

She will probably work in a dreary factory her entire life and never have a family of her own.

It would have been rude, and embarrassing to Anya, to tell Leah that I was feeling just fine until Dmitri, and then she, had shown up, so all I said was, "I'm all right," and we started walking again.

The city was bustling with noisy activity as the four of us continued on to the Asch building. Laundry hung from fire escapes and across the railings of balconies above storefronts. Cart horses clomped down the busy streets, creating clouds of dust. Stalls loaded with fruits, vegetables, clothing, black bread, pretzels, and all kinds of other goods for sale, were crowded together along the roadway.

I heard a peddler with a pushcart, yell out, "Shoelaces! Shoelaces!" as he hawked his wares.

The *Clang! Clang! Clang!* of a fire wagon's bell sounded in the distance. It seemed there was always a fire burning some place in this huge city and a horse-drawn fire wagon racing along to put out the fire.

The Lower East Side was a mixture of many different immigrant groups, but I always heard at least a few people speaking Yiddish as we made our way to work each morning. This made me feel safe. In Russia, we had lived in a tiny farmhouse within a small village. Here, in New York, it was almost as if that village had been transplanted to a space inside this large city, which made the city seem less foreign. The main difference was that instead of farms and scattered villages dotting the landscape as they did in Russia, our homes here were among the towering tenements that reached to the sky.

Eventually, the four of us came to the Asch building, which stood at the corner of Greene Street and Washington Place. It was a light brown and reddish clay-colored structure, ten stories high, and only a block from a beautiful park. Several signs on the corner of the building advertised the various businesses that were housed inside. The Triangle Shirtwaist Company was not the only clothing factory in this building, but there was one big difference between the Triangle Shirtwaist Company and the others there. Triangle was the only company that was not a union shop. That meant it did not knowingly hire union workers nor operate according to union practices or restrictions.

The Asch building had another important distinction. It was considered fireproof because it was made mostly of stone. That was probably the reason we never had fire drills. Plus, most of the workers in the building did not even realize there was a fire escape because it was concealed behind a pair of metal shutters that I never saw opened. The only reason I knew about the fire escape was because I tried to open the shutters one day and someone told me what was behind them.

As we approached the building now, Dmitri whispered something in Anya's ear. She giggled and whispered back to him.

"Come on, Dmitri," said Leah. "Tear yourself away from Anya now so we can get to work."

Dmitri smiled sheepishly, then he and Leah said good-bye to us and they started off down the street again.

Anya pulled me along. "Come, Little Shadow . . . we'll be late."

Although the Asch building had two passenger elevators inside the front entrance to the building on the Washington Place side, workers for the Triangle Shirtwaist Company were not allowed to use them or the front entrance. We were only permitted to use the stairs or the freight elevators, which were on the Greene Street side of the building. Many of the girls were afraid of the elevators and always used the stairs. Anya and I didn't mind taking an elevator. It was much easier and faster than walking up to the eighth floor.

As usual, this morning we entered the freight elevator.

"Good morning, ladies," said Joseph Zito, the elevator operator.

"Good morning," Anya and I both said to him. Joseph was a kind man who seemed to enjoy his job, although it couldn't have been very exciting going up and down in an elevator so many times each day. He closed the wire fencing that served as a door for the elevator, and we moved slowly up to the eighth floor, where I got out.

The Asch building was a loft building, which meant each floor was one huge room with a very high ceiling. On each floor of the Triangle Shirtwaist Company, wooden partitions had been built to make washrooms and changing rooms for the workers. We never spent much time in either of those places, however. If our supervisor felt we had been in the washroom too long, she would threaten to dock our pay, or sometimes even fire us. I did not let that bother me, though. As long as I knew what to expect, I could follow the rules and stay out of trouble.

"Say good morning to Rebecca for me," I called out to Anya, who remained in the elevator to continue on to the ninth floor, where she worked alongside our friend Rebecca and hundreds of other girls.

As the elevator car moved up, and Anya was soon out of sight, I headed for the dressing room to hang up my coat and scarf before starting work. Two of my friends, Mary and Minnie, were already in there, giggling and whispering about something. Mary was always so bright and cheerful. I never saw her in a gloomy mood. When she noticed me she said, "You'd better hurry, Galena. We're going to be late if we don't get to our places right away."

Mary, Minnie, and I were thread cutters. Mary was the same age as me, barely eleven. Minnie was a year or so older. Along with several other of the youngest girls in the factory, we sat on stools, next to stacks of garments in a corner of the room. Here we worked for the entire day, clipping threads from garments as the operators sewed them. We were actually too young to be working in a factory such as the Triangle Shirtwaist Company, but city inspectors did not have time to visit the factories very often. And the factory owners were more than happy to hire us because they could pay us less than they would have to pay older, more experienced workers. If a city inspector showed up during the day, the owners or supervisors hid us in some crates or in one of the elevators until the inspector left the building.

Minnie's older sister, Celia, who was almost eighteen, worked on the eighth floor with us, too. Since she was older and more experienced than any of us, she was an operator and worked at one of the many sewing machines on the long tables lined up across the room.

Because it was almost time for the workday to begin, the floor supervisor stood ready to give the signal for "power on." Soon the sewing machines would start up with a flash of needles, and the whole floor would vibrate with the roar and whir of them all.

The eighth floor was a busy and interesting place. Yet I dreamed of working on the ninth floor with Anya. Sometimes I would go there during lunchtime and we would eat together. The ninth floor was crowded with eight long tables that held dozens of sewing machines, which were lined up on both sides of each table. That meant there were two rows of chairs between each of the tables, so it was difficult for girls at the machines in the middle of the tables to get out of their aisles unless the other girls scooted in their chairs. I often thought that it would be so much easier just to stand on the tables and walk across them, but that was not allowed. Besides, it would not be very ladylike to walk across the tables. Yet, I thought it would be a lot of fun to do.

Even though the rooms of each floor of the Asch building were quite large, they were all very cluttered. Under the tables on each floor were bins of fabric scraps, and rags dampened by sewing machine oil. Many of these remnants were of a material called lawn, which was very flimsy and highly flammable. Paper patterns hung on wires, like clotheslines, stretched out overhead across the entire length of the room on the eighth and ninth floors. The walls of each floor of the Triangle Shirtwaist Company were lined with small metal buckets filled with water. These buckets could be used to put out small fires that often sparked up among the fabric due to a careless flick of a cigar or a cigarette.

Very little sunlight entered the rooms, so gaslights on the wall were always lit; yet workers still had to strain to guide the cloth under the sewing machine needles in the dim light of these lamps.

During my first few months at the Triangle Shirtwaist Company, my eyes burned from the strong dyes in the fabrics. I coughed a lot from the tiny bits of lint that entered my lungs whenever I took a breath. But now, I was used to the dyes in the cloth, so my eyes didn't water every time I entered the factory. I still coughed occasionally, but sometimes I tied my scarf around my neck and tucked it inside the top of my dress so I could pull it up over my nose if I found I was inhaling too many bits of lint.

Surprisingly, even though the huge room where I worked was dark, cluttered, and without fresh air, I enjoyed being with the other girls there. Our floor supervisor was strict and unkind, but as long as we arrived on time and worked quickly, we did not have to worry. We were not bothered very often.

I glanced up at the sewing machines. The operator of each one quickly guided cut fabric underneath the threaded needle, producing a line of straight stitching that bound two parts of a garment together. As the bound pieces left the sewing machine, they fell into a trough in

between the rows of tables. The work at Triangle was a very systematic process, which was almost beautiful in a way, except the operators were sometimes pushed to work so quickly that they'd run the sewing machine needle straight through their fingers instead of the cloth. When that happened, a girl did not complain. She just wrapped her fingers in a piece of cloth and kept working. She could not afford to get behind in the number of garments she was supposed to finish by the end of the day.

In addition to the operators, there were all kinds of different jobs in the factory. Some people were cutters. They used large, sharp scissors to cut through layers of fabric to make the pieces that would be the sleeves, backs, and fronts, of the shirtwaists. Other workers added intricate embroidery to the fronts of the blouses. There were also many male tailors on our floor. I did not know all of them because there were so many. But I did know one. His name was Max Rother. He was a very nice man who would smile and say hello whenever he saw me. I appreciated the way he acknowledged me, since many of the other adult workers there never seemed to notice a simple thread cutter like me.

On the tenth floor, which was where the offices for the factory were, along with the showroom and the finishing room for garments, finishers would make the final touches to each of the blouses, then press them so they were more presentable and each seam was set. But no matter what kind of job a worker at the Triangle Shirtwaist Company was hired to do, the work was always done very, very quickly.

We followed our morning routine, as usual. When it was time for lunch I scurried upstairs to enjoy some time on the ninth floor with Anya and Rebecca. Mary and Minnie went with me.

"I'll be up there in a few minutes," Celia called out to us as we headed for the stairs. "I have to do something first."

Anya and Rebecca were already seated in the corner, unwrapping their lunches by the time Mary, Minnie, and I got upstairs.

"It's still a bit chilly to eat outside in the park," said Anya when she saw us. She shivered and pulled her shawl around her shoulders. "In fact, I'd love a cup of hot tea right now."

Rebecca rolled her eyes as she unwrapped a chunk of dark bread from some newsprint. "Well, I suppose we'd have to buy our lunches at a coffee shop if we wanted something hot to drink," she said. "And I know I don't have money to waste on such things as hot tea or a fancy meal in the middle of the day."

Mary laughed. "Oh, Rebecca, you're always so sensible. Don't you ever do anything that's impractical and just plain fun?"

Rebecca seemed to be studying the question for a moment. Finally she said, "No, I guess I don't." Then she took a bite of bread while everyone laughed at her complete honesty.

"Where's Celia?" asked Rebecca. "Isn't she going to join us for lunch?"

"She'll be here in a few minutes," I answered. "She said she had to do something first."

I saw Minnie and Mary exchange a look.

"What's going on with Celia?" I asked them. "I can tell you both know why she's late for lunch."

Anya did not give either of them a chance to answer. "Not that it's any business of yours Little Shadow, since you wouldn't be the slightest bit interested. But Celia is telling some of the girls about a special meeting that will take place tonight. Leah is going to explain how the union operates. Celia is trying to get as many girls to come to the meeting as she can."

Minnie nodded, then she spoke softly, as if she didn't want to be overheard. "And it isn't easy to spread the word in a nonunion shop. Celia would be fired if the foremen found out she was encouraging workers to go to a union meeting."

"Well, she's a brave girl," said Anya. "And the union will continue to get stronger and stronger as long as there are brave girls like Celia around."

Mary looked over at Anya. "Does that mean you'll be attending this meeting tonight?" she asked.

Anya looked over at me and hesitated.

"No, it doesn't mean that," I said before Anya could answer. "Mama doesn't want Anya joining the union, so she doesn't need to find out how it operates."

Just then Celia rushed in with her lunch. "Whew!" she said. "I thought I'd never finish in time to join you. But I had something important to do."

Rebecca smiled at her. "We know, Celia. Anya told us."

Celia dragged a chair over and sat down next to Anya. "Then you know this won't be an official meeting. Leah just wants to answer some questions many girls have about the union."

"That's wonderful," said Mary. "I'd be too afraid to ask questions if there were official union leaders there."

"So come and ask your questions to Leah tonight," said Celia.

"No one told me about this meeting," I said. "Why is that?"

Celia chuckled. "What's the point, Galena? Everyone knows you'll never join the union because of your mama.

Besides, if Triangle followed union rules you wouldn't be working here. You're just a child. You should be in school."

I stood up. "Don't tell me where I should be, Celia. And I have every right to find out about the union. I'll be old enough to join some day."

"Be quiet, Galena," Anya whispered. "If the foreman hears you, we'll all be out looking for new jobs."

I plopped back down in my seat. I did not want to make us all lose our jobs. But I did not want to feel left out of things among my friends either. Yet there was not time to discuss this anymore at the moment. We had to get back to work.

Celia and Minnie started to the stairway. Mary waited for me.

"I need to talk to Anya," I told Mary. "I'll be downstairs in a minute."

I followed Anya to the dressing area where she placed her shawl back on the hook that held her coat and scarf. I moved close beside her so no one could hear me ask, "Are you planning on attending that meeting tonight, Anya?"

Anya put her hands on her hips. "Yes, Little Shadow, as a matter of fact, I am."

I did not quite know what to say. Anya had never disobeyed Mama. At least, not as far as I knew.

"But what about Mama?" I asked.

"I'm not going to tell her," said Anya. "She thinks I'm going over to Celia's to help her with a dress she is making for Minnie. And that's partially true. I will be doing that before I go to the meeting. Mama just doesn't need to know *everything* I plan on doing tonight."

"Then I'm going with you," I said.

Anya shook her head. "No!" she said. "I will find out about the union. If I decide to join, I will. Then, once Mama has learned to accept that, and you are older, you can join yourself, if you like." She scooted me along. "Now, get back downstairs before you're late for work."

"Hmph," I said, then I hurried down the stairs and jumped on my stool just as the sewing machines all started up again.

Yet, I couldn't get the union meeting out of my mind all afternoon. If Anya was going to that meeting, I wanted to go, too.

Don't I have a right to know what's going on if it means I might lose my job someday soon? I wondered.

At quitting time we all lined up at the Washington Place side of the building to have our purses inspected before we were allowed to leave for the day. It never seemed fair that the men just waltzed out of the building without having their jacket pockets searched. Every woman and girl in the factory had to open her purse to

prove she wasn't trying to make off with a bit of fabric or thread or something else that she hadn't paid for.

Dmitri was on the sidewalk waiting for us, as usual, when we came out of the building. Leah was with him. Many of the girls from the factory gathered around the two of them. Finally, they cleared away and Dmitri walked over to Anya and took her hand.

Minnie and Mary smiled and looked at me as if to say, "Anya and Dmitri are courting."

But I was sure they were wrong if they thought that.

Dmitri was simply trying to convince Anya to join the union.

I bet he won't be interested in her at all anymore once she joins.

Mary moved beside me and looped her arm through mine. "Why don't you come to the meeting tonight?" she asked me. "If your mother won't let you and Anya go alone, then ask her to come with the two of you."

Mary just did not understand Mama.

"It's no use, Mary. Mama will never agree to let Anya join the union. If Anya goes to that meeting tonight she'll be deliberately defying her."

Mary looked thoughtful. Finally she said, "Well, maybe Anya should defy your mama if it's for something good. Maybe that's why Anya is willing to disobey your mother now. I know I'll join the union when I'm older."

"Yeah, when you're older. Right now the union could cause you to lose your job! Have you thought about that?"

"Yes, I have," said Mary. "And if workers were paid more for their labor, then so many of us who are underage wouldn't have to work. Just think about that, Galena. If Anya made more money, you could go to school because your family wouldn't need your salary so badly right now."

But I want to help my family by earning a salary.

I pulled away from Mary and folded my arms across my chest. "Well, maybe you're right about the union, Mary. But Anya still should not disobey Mama. She's only doing that because Dmitri is persuading her to do it. I don't trust him, and I wish Anya would stay away from him."

But even as I said it, I knew Anya would probably never stay away from Dmitri.

chapter three

I Sneak Out
to Find Anya

That evening I cleared the table after supper and Mama washed the dishes. Anya had already told Mama she was going to Celia's later to help Celia make a dress for Minnie.

"Is Celia making a *special* dress for Minnie?" Mama asked as Anya dried the plates and put them in the cupboard.

I looked at Anya, waiting to hear how she would answer Mama's question.

Will you tell Mama the whole truth, Anya? And aren't you afraid that I might tell Mama about the union meeting you plan to attend tonight, too?

"Minnie's birthday is next week," said Anya. "The dress is to be a surprise birthday present."

Anya looked at me. I could tell she was trying to figure out whether or not I would betray her by telling Mama about the union meeting.

I gave her a reassuring look.

Mama smiled. "Isn't Celia nice? She and Minnie are such close sisters. Just like you two."

I smiled weakly, thinking that I did not want to be so close to my sister if it meant I had to keep secrets from Mama.

Anya put down the dish towel. "Yes, they're very close," she said. "But I need to leave now. Leah is going with me to help Celia with the dress. I promised I'd meet Leah downstairs in a few minutes."

I turned to Mama. "Can I go with Anya, Mama? Please, I'd like to visit Minnie."

Anya gave me a stern look. "You silly girl. Minnie won't be home tonight," she said. "It wouldn't be a surprise if she saw us sewing her dress, now would it? Her mother has taken her to see a play."

I made a face at Anya. I did not believe for a second that Minnie's mother was taking her to see a play. Anya had just quickly created that part of her story, adding another lie to her tale.

Mama pulled me to her and gave me a hug. "Stay here and keep me company, Galena."

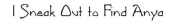

"All right," I said, feeling guilty that I had just considered disobeying Mama, too.

Mama gave me a kiss on the forehead.

Anya looked out the front window, then took her coat and scarf from the peg by the door.

"Leah is downstairs now, so I'd better go. You don't need to wait up for me," she said to Mama. "We told Celia we would help her finish the dress tonight, so it will probably be a few hours before I return."

"Don't worry about us," I said, standing with my hands on my hips now. "Mama and I will be just fine."

I turned away from Mama so she could not see my face as I stuck out my tongue at Anya before she left the apartment.

After Anya closed the door, I went to the window and looked out.

Leah was down on the sidewalk all right. Dmitri was with her.

Hmm . . . Anya didn't tell Mama that Dmitri would be joining them this evening. I knew he was a bad influence on Anya. Before she met Dmitri, Anya never lied to Mama.

"Come away from the window, Galena," said Mama. "Help me plan the Sabbath dinner for tomorrow night."

I turned from the window and took an apron from a peg on the wall. Dinner on Friday evenings was always the

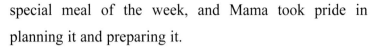

special meal of the week, and Mama took pride in planning it and preparing it.

"I'll start the challah," I told her.

I knew Mama would have the eggs and other ingredients needed for the two loaves of rich egg bread that we usually enjoyed as part of our Sabbath dinner. Since this bread took a while to prepare, we always started it on Thursday evening so it would have time to rise before Mama baked it the next day.

I carefully combined all the ingredients. Then, as I kneaded the bread, Mama showed me some delicious-looking spring greens she had bought at the market.

"We'll have these for our Sabbath supper tomorrow night, too," she said proudly, just as Papa opened the door and came in from work. "And I'll go to the fish market tomorrow when I take a break at noon for lunch, so we'll have fresh fish for the Sabbath meal, too."

Papa pulled off his hat and coat and laid them on the dresser next to the door.

"Wash up," said Mama. "Your supper is still warm."

Papa went to the kitchen sink and washed and dried his hands, then he sat down at the table.

Mama set a plate of food before him.

"Where's Anya?" Papa asked.

I felt like answering, "She's at the union hall with Leah and Dmitri!" But I did not say a word, I just kept kneading the bread dough.

"She went to a friend's house to help with some sewing," said Mama.

Papa stabbed some beans with his fork and raised the fork to his mouth. "Hasn't she sewn enough for one day?" he asked before he ate the beans.

Mama stood next to him and put her hands on his shoulders. "Ah . . . but that sewing was for work. This sewing is for fun."

Papa looked at me. "Has Anya said anything more about joining the union?" he asked.

I froze.

Does he somehow know that Anya has gone to a union meeting?

Mama went to the stove and grabbed the pot of beans. She spooned more beans onto Papa's plate. "She talked about the union the other morning," said Mama in Yiddish. "Why do you ask?"

Papa looked up at Mama sheepishly. "Maybe the union is not such a bad idea," he said. "I would be ready to join if it meant I could get home in time for supper with my family."

Mama stood with her hands on her hips, looking at Papa. She didn't say anything, so Papa kept eating and did

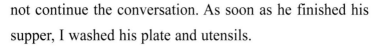

not continue the conversation. As soon as he finished his supper, I washed his plate and utensils.

"Well, time for bed," said Papa. "I am very tired this evening. I will see you tomorrow, Galena." He looked at Mama. "Come to bed soon, my dear."

He kissed the top of my head, then walked to the middle of the room and drew the curtain.

"Mama, why don't you go to bed early tonight, too. I can finish up here. You look tired as well," I said.

Mama took off her apron, folded it neatly and put it on the table. "Yes, I am a bit tired tonight," she said. "But I think I should stay up and wait for Anya."

I prodded Mama toward the curtain. "I'll wait up for her. I have a book so I'll read until she gets home."

Mama yawned. "All right then," she said. "Be sure to turn out the lamp when the two of you come to bed."

"I will, Mama. Good night."

Mama eased behind the curtain to the sleeping area of the room so she would change her clothes and slip into bed beside Papa.

I braided the challah, then wrapped it in a dish towel and left it beside the stove in a warm place where it would rise. Mama would bake it tomorrow afternoon, once the other ladies who worked with her had left our apartment for the day.

I sat down at the table and opened my book. It was a simple book because my English was not so good. But I could not concentrate on the words on the pages. I kept thinking about Anya.

I just don't trust Dmitri. I need to keep Anya safe from him.

I listened for Mama's soft breathing and Papa's loud snores.

Good. They're both asleep.

I eased open the door to our apartment and walked out to the hallway, then closed the door softly.

I'm sorry, Mama. I don't want to disobey you. But I have to protect Anya. Dmitri will talk her into doing something she might not really want to do, and I can't let that happen.

I tiptoed down the stairs quickly and ran out the door, then raced to the union hall. Luckily, I had heard the other girls talk about the hall often enough so that I knew exactly where it was. Once I got there I swallowed hard, then opened the door and walked in.

There were only a few girls there besides Celia, Anya, and Leah. Leah and Dmitri were seated in the front of the room. Leah was addressing the audience, but everyone turned to look at me when they heard the door open.

"Galena!" Anya said excitedly. "What are you doing here?" She rushed over to me.

"I came to find out what the union is all about," I told her.

"Then come sit down and join us," Leah called from the front of the room. "I will tell you."

Dmitri was polite enough to stand up as I took an empty seat in front of him. He smiled at me, but I just glared at him.

Anya sat down beside me. "Does Mama know you're here?"

"No," I said. "But she doesn't know you're here either."

"You shouldn't have disobeyed Mama," whispered Anya.

"Neither should you," I whispered back.

Anya could not argue with that, so she gave up. We sat quietly and listened while Leah told us about the union. Everything Leah said made sense. All the girls wanted to work in cleaner, safer factories. And everyone wanted better pay and fewer hours.

Mary was seated behind me. "The union does sound like a good thing. Doesn't it, Galena?" she said once Leah had stopped talking.

I nodded. "Yes, but it also sounds like it can be dangerous. I mean . . . we could get fired. We're not even supposed to be working at our age."

When Leah had finished, Anya turned to me and said, "Go home now, Galena. Mary and Minnie will walk with you. Dmitri wants to talk to me about something."

I glared at her. "You've decided to join the union, haven't you?" I said. "That's what Dmitri is going to talk to you about. Does Papa know you're here?"

Anya looked surprised. "Of course Papa doesn't know I'm here," she said. Then she smiled and pulled me to her. "Don't worry, Little Shadow. I will talk to Mama again before I join anything. Go home now. I'll be there soon."

The next morning at breakfast Mama was anxious to find out about Minnie's dress.

"Did you finish the dress last night?" she asked Anya.

I stared at Anya, wondering if she would tell Mama the entire truth about where she had been last night.

"Yes, Mama. We did," said Anya. "And the dress is beautiful. Minnie will be so surprised and happy."

Mama sat down at the table and sipped her tea. She looked at me. "And where were you last night, Miss Galena Borchek?"

I nearly choked on a sip of tea. When I stopped coughing I said, "What do you mean, Mama? I was here with you and Papa."

Anya did not say a word.

Mama looked at me sternly. "I woke up last night and did not see you in your bed or reading at the table. Did you follow your sister after all?"

I gulped and thought quickly. "No, Mama. I was out on the fire escape, just thinking. I like to watch the city lights at night, you know that."

I often went out onto the fire escape to be alone, so it would not be difficult for Mama to believe that I had been out there last night.

"I see," said Mama. "Well, don't leave the apartment anymore when I am asleep . . . not even to go out onto the fire escape."

Does she know I'm not telling her the truth?

My palms grew sweaty.

I hate lying to people, especially to Mama.

"Yes, Mama," I said.

Mama turned to Anya. "I'm glad you finished the dress for Minnie, Anya. Now . . . the two of you need to get to work."

Anya and I got up from the table and put on our coats and scarves and left the apartment.

I did not mention the union meeting to Anya again. I did not want to cause an argument so early in the morning and start off the day badly with her.

Before we stepped outside I said, "Bubbie. I want to see Bubbie's photograph, Anya."

Anya pushed open the door. "You need to stop these childish behaviors, Galena. You don't need to see Bubbie's photograph every morning before you go to work. Come on. It's time to meet Dmitri."

Anya stepped outside onto the sidewalk.

I could not seem to follow her. My mind was suddenly racing with questions.

Has something happened to the locket? You promised Bubbie you would never remove it, Anya. Has Dmitri persuaded you to sell it to pay union dues or something? Why in the world would you refuse to let me see it?

For the first time in my life, Anya seemed like a stranger to me.

And Dmitri was perhaps more horrible than I had even imagined. He had caused Anya to disobey Mama and to lie to her. And I was no better than Anya. I had done the exact same awful things, thanks to him.

That night after work I set the table for the Sabbath meal. Mama had already lit the Sabbath candles by the time Anya and I returned from work since Papa would not be home until after sundown. Sabbath candles should always be lit before sundown. When Papa did get home from work, we gathered around the table to sing Shalom Aleichem (Peace to You) and offered the Sabbath blessings. After the meal, we sang more songs, then walked to the synagogue for the Sabbath prayer service.

After the service, when Anya and I were back home in our bed, I whispered to her, "I don't feel right, Anya. We both defied Mama this week. And we lied to her, too."

Anya rolled over to face me. "I don't feel good about those things either, Galena. But it will all work out for the best. You'll see. We didn't defy Mama or lie to her for some foolish or mean reason. We did it for the good of all the girls who work in the factories."

"I guess so," I agreed. "But what did you talk to Dmitri about last night after the meeting?"

Anya smiled. "Nothing you need to be concerned about, Little Shadow. Now go to sleep."

Anya closed her eyes and was soon breathing peacefully.

But I could not sleep. I kept thinking about her meeting with Dmitri.

Will I ever find out their secret? I wondered. *And what happened to the locket? Did Dmitri ask her to sell it for some reason?*

chapter four

My Life Changes Forever

The next morning as Anya and I walked downstairs to the front door of our apartment building, I tugged at my sister's sleeve.

"May I see Bubbie's photograph now, please? I don't care if it is a childish request, Anya. I want to see it. You know it makes me feel better, and I have a happier day when I have seen Bubbie and have said good-bye to Papa and Mama in the photograph."

"There's no time for that now, Galena," Anya said sternly. "Besides, they are only photographs in a locket. It's not like you will never see Mama and Papa again."

But we'll never see Bubbie again . . . why are you being so disagreeable about this every morning now, Anya?

I wanted to ask her if she had sold or lost the locket. But both of those possibilities were almost unthinkable, so, as we stepped outside, I decided to ignore Anya's unusual behavior. I looked up at the beautiful sky and tried to push all unpleasant thoughts from my mind and enjoy the gorgeous spring morning. Plus, Saturday was payday at the Triangle Shirtwaist Company. I was looking forward to receiving my pay envelope at the end of the day. Months ago, Anya and I had begged Mama to let us start saving a few pennies of our salary each payday so we could each buy a new hat by spring. At first, Mama told us we were being selfish to want to spend money on ourselves. But when she saw other young ladies wearing hats, she realized we just wanted to look more respectable than we did in our old cotton scarves from Russia, so she gave in to our begging. And now I could hardly wait to buy my new hat.

Anya chatted with Dmitri as I glided along, arm in arm with her, trying to ignore him as much as possible. I was lost in thought, daydreaming about the new hat I would soon purchase. At long last I would have enough money for it.

Anya reached over and smoothed back my hair. "What are you thinking about, Little Shadow? With such a big smile on your face, it must be happy thoughts."

Dmitri chuckled. "She's probably thinking about what she will do tomorrow because it is Sunday and she won't have to work at the factory," he said. "I know what we should do, Anya. We should have a picnic."

Anya smiled. "That's a lovely idea. And you will join us, of course, Galena."

My happy thoughts vanished, but I tried not to frown. The last thing in the world I wanted to do was spend my one and only day off with Dmitri and have to share my sister with him.

Oh, why did things have to change? My life was nearly perfect before Anya met this bossy man.

Yet I knew I would join them for the picnic tomorrow. It was the only way I would get to spend time with my precious sister.

Anya pulled away from me and approached one of the pushcarts on the street.

"Ah . . . pickles," she said.

She opened her pocketbook and removed a few coins to exchange them for two large pickles, which she wrapped in the newsprint that held our lunch. She inhaled the newsprint deeply.

"I love the briny, dill smell of pickles," she said. "These will be delicious for our lunch today, Galena."

Dmitri took Anya by the arm. "We don't have time to talk about pickles," he said. "We must not be late for work." He pulled Anya along.

As we approached the Asch building, I thought about what Anya had said the other day about union members. We would be the only workers in the building this afternoon. The other businesses would all stop work at noon today because they were all union shops. Although I did not believe in the union, I could not help but be a little jealous.

Oh, how lucky the union workers are. They can enjoy the afternoon in the sunshine today, but we'll still be inside sewing.

Later, when we were working, I stared at the dirty windows. I had a bad case of spring fever, even though it was only March 25, which meant spring had barely begun. If we could not be outside to enjoy the sunshine today, I wished we could at least admire the bright and beautiful day through the windows. But they were grimy and blocked out most of the sunlight. They were always kept closed anyway because the factory owners were afraid we would steal fabric by tossing it out the window, or that we would get distracted from our work by the noises out on the street below. Instead of gentle spring breezes circulating across the room, we inhaled the strong dyes in the fabrics, sewing machine oil, and eventually the sweat of those working next to us.

I'll have to wait until lunchtime to get a breath of fresh air today.

I knew we would not be allowed to eat our lunches out on the fire escape either because a few weeks ago I had asked if we could eat our lunch there and was told the fire escape was too flimsy. However, we could walk over to the park, even though we'd only have a short time to enjoy our food in the warm sunshine. I began to look forward to that and smiled.

Mary noticed me smiling and smiled back.

I made a motion as if I were eating something with a fork and mouthed the word "outside," hoping the foreman wouldn't see me. We were not allowed to talk to one another as we worked. We were not supposed to sing either. But the sewing machines made so much noise that sometimes I gently hummed, just loudly enough that I was the only one to hear it. It lifted my spirits and made the time pass more quickly.

All the operators were working furiously now. Our foreman walked over to Mary, picked up a garment from the stack next to her and shoved it at her. "Get to work, girl. You think we're paying you to sit here and smile?"

Mary's smile instantly disappeared, and she hurriedly checked the garment for loose threads and snipped them off with her scissors.

I snipped loose threads from another garment in the pile, then reached for another, working as quickly as I could.

The foreman nodded and walked away.

By lunchtime, when the sewing machines all came to a sudden halt and the room was instantly alive with chatter, my back ached from sitting hunched over the garments in my lap all morning. I was eager to take a break and stretch outside in the sunshine. Anya came down to our floor to join Mary, Minnie, Celia, and me for lunch. The four of us were prepared to drag Anya to the stairway if she insisted on eating inside.

"Let's eat outside in the park today, Anya," I said, as I got behind her and started to gently push her toward the stairway. But it did not take much prodding to get her to agree to eat outdoors. The five of us filed down the stairs and made our way to the ground floor.

When we stepped outside the building onto the sidewalk, Mary lifted her face up to the sky and closed her eyes. "What a glorious day to be alive," she said, sounding so much older than she really was. "Breathe in the sweet smells of spring while you can, girls."

We all inhaled deeply, then coughed and giggled as a horse and cart passed by, kicking up a cloud of dust and leaving a less than pleasant aroma behind.

"Come on, you silly girls!" said Minnie. "I'm starving. Let's eat. We haven't much time."

We crossed the street and walked to Washington Square, a large park a block away from the Asch building.

There we spread our coats and scarves onto the warm grass. The park was beautiful, with a huge stone arch that looked just like one in Paris that I had seen in a magazine.

We can sit in the park and imagine we are lunching in Paris without a care in the world.

Anya unfolded the newsprint that surrounded hunks of bread, two slices of cheese, and the pickles she had bought earlier from one of the pushcarts. She set the paper on the ground and said, "Take some bread and cheese, Little Shadow, and don't forget to try one of these tasty pickles."

I reached for a slice of cheese and put it on the bread. Although it was nothing but a simple lunch, and the same foods I ate every day, I was so hungry that the creamy cheese and the rich bread were most delicious. When I finished all of the bread and cheese, I reached for a pickle and tasted it.

My mouth puckered and everyone laughed.

"Sour, huh?" asked Minnie.

I nodded. "Uh-huh."

Mary, Minnie, and Celia had unwrapped their lunches and spread the papers out on the grass. Everyone was happily munching away on her food, even though none of us had anything very fancy to eat.

"It's the perfect day for a picnic," said Mary. "This is so much fun."

Anya lay back in the grass, leisurely enjoying her lunch. "Actually, tomorrow will be more perfect for a picnic because we won't have to work."

"And Anya and I *are* going on a picnic tomorrow," I said to Mary.

"Just the two of you?" she asked.

I frowned as Anya sat up and said, "Of course not, silly. Dmitri is going with us."

Celia looked at me. "You really are Anya's 'Little Shadow,' aren't you, Galena?"

Mary and Minnie giggled.

I made a face and said, "Dmitri . . . ugh!"

"Stop it, Galena," said Anya. "I know Dmitri is not your favorite person. But he is a good man and you should not be so unkind toward him."

Mary touched Anya's arm. "My, my, Anya, you certainly are protective of Dmitri. Is he courting you now?"

Anya brushed Mary's hand away. "Why, Miss Mary Goldstein, you are quite the nosy little lady today, aren't you? Well, if Dmitri is courting me it's no business of yours."

"Of course Dmitri is not courting her!" I blurted out. "Mama has hired a shadchen to find the perfect husband for Anya. In fact, she will meet her possible match next week."

Anya's face paled. "Don't be so sure of that, Galena," she muttered. "Maybe I want to choose my own match, without the help of a shadchen."

Mary lay back in the grass. "Of course you do," she said dreamily. "It would be much better to marry someone you truly love. Wouldn't it?"

"That's the American way, after all," agreed Minnie. "And that's what I intend to do when I'm older. I don't care what my parents say."

"But Mama doesn't do things the American way," I reminded everyone. "And Anya *does* care what Mama and Papa say. Don't you, Anya?"

I prayed that I was right about that, and Anya really did still care what Mama and Papa said. But I was not so sure anymore, especially now that Anya had disobeyed and lied to Mama. When Anya did not answer for several moments I became nervous. Finally she said, "Yes, I do care what they say. But we're in America now, and people here are expected to do things the American way. Mama and Papa may need to change their Old World ways, Galena."

"Who will need to change their Old World ways?" asked a familiar voice.

I looked up to see Rebecca standing before us. Rebecca was also a Russian Jew who had been in America for only a short time. She was not a beautiful girl, like Anya. But she was attractive. At least she would have been if she had taken the time to try to look her best. Unlike so many of the other girls, Rebecca did not dress in the popular shirtwaists. She adhered to the strict religious ways and still wore the clothes she had brought with her from Russia. They were not very colorful or fashionable, but they made Rebecca instantly recognizable. She definitely did not blend in with the rest of the girls at the Triangle Shirtwaist Company, but she did not seem to care.

"Anya's mother, Mrs. Borchek," answered Mary, before either Anya or I had a chance to say anything.

Rebecca laughed. "Jewish parents do not change so easily," she said. "Just because Anya now lives in America does not mean she will be allowed to choose her own husband without the help of a shadchen."

I patted the ground beside me. "Come join us, Rebecca."

Maybe I should encourage Anya to spend more time with Rebecca and she will realize she might as well lose interest in Dmitri. He is not the perfect match for her. He's only interested in her as another recruit for the union anyway.

We talked and giggled and ate together for a while longer, as if we were having a party. Our lovely picnic passed quickly. Before we knew it, it was time to return to the dark, cluttered world of the factory.

"I hate to go back to work," said Rebecca. "It is so beautiful out here."

Anya stood up and shook bread crumbs and grass from her coat. "It won't be so bad," she told her. "I've heard we will have cake this afternoon to celebrate the engagement of one of the girls. That means you will have something to look forward to before the work day is over, Rebecca."

There were so many engaged girls at the Triangle Shirtwaist Company. Almost every week another girl would join the ranks of the soon to be wed and flash a shiny ring in our faces, which was the custom among excited immigrant girls.

Rebecca's face brightened. "M-m-m . . . cake!"

"Another engagement," said Mary. "How romantic."

Anya smiled. "Yes, it is romantic." She turned to Rebecca. "No shadchen found this girl's match either. Her fiancé is exactly her age—not some tired-looking older man—and she is madly in love with him. She told me so."

I groaned. Mama had explained this kind of "mad love" to me. In fact, she said it was not really love at all. It was something called infatuation, although Mama had used a Yiddish word, but I asked someone else what it meant and they had told me it meant infatuation, which is not really love. It is just a sudden attraction to someone. Mama said that real love was more than an attraction and it developed over time. I felt Mama should know because she had met Papa through a shadchen in Russia when she was just Anya's age, and the two of them had married and grown to love each other deeply over the years. That was what Mama wanted for Anya now. True love that would develop over time. Not just some infatuation with a handsome man who wanted Anya to join the union.

Rebecca laughed. "Then this girl must not be Jewish," she said.

"You're as bad as Mama, Rebecca!" Anya frowned and turned to leave the park.

As we made our way back to the Asch building, we passed workers from the other clothing companies who were on their way home.

"We would be going home now, too, if the Triangle was a union factory," Anya whispered to me.

I rolled my eyes. "But Triangle is not a union factory," I whispered back angrily, "so there is no use wishing for something that is not so. Besides, if Triangle were a union factory and followed the rules, I wouldn't be working there at all, so stop wishing for such things!"

"You wouldn't *have* to work there if I earned better wages," said Anya. "I'd make enough money to help the family and you could go to school."

I stuck out my tongue at her.

I don't want to go to school!

Anya huffed, then she and Rebecca hurried back up to the ninth floor.

Once on the eighth floor, Mary, Minnie, Celia, and I stopped in the dressing area to leave our coats.

We worked steadily all afternoon. Around four o'clock our names were called, one by one, as pay envelopes were distributed. When I received mine I could not resist opening it and admiring my earnings.

Twelve dollars for two weeks work. Mama will be so happy and I will get to buy my new hat. I certainly wouldn't earn twelve dollars every two weeks for going to school. So I hope you forget about the silly old union, Anya. I want to keep my job!

I closed my pay envelope and stuffed it into the collar of my dress since I had no pockets. Then I got back to work.

When I glanced up at the clock it was almost four thirty. I swiftly cut loose threads from a few more garments, but my mind was not on my work.

Anya and the other girls on the ninth floor are probably enjoying delicious cake right now. They're so lucky. Nothing exciting ever happens down here on the eighth floor.

A few minutes later, I glanced at the clock on the wall again. It was 4:45 and the bell rang to signal "power off." All at once the sewing machines stopped. There was a split second of near silence before everyone started chattering, and the room was filled with laughter, talk, and the sounds of chairs being shoved away from, then back under, the tables that held the sewing machines.

Girls lined up at the Greene Street side to have their pocketbooks inspected on their way out, even though the door to the stairway was not open yet. As usual, the owners wanted to make certain we were not trying to steal a bit of cloth or a small garment from the factory. Only then would we be allowed to file down the stairs.

I gathered my coat from the dressing area. I took my pay envelope from my dress and stuffed it into my coat pocket, then carried my coat back out to the main room. I left Mary, Minnie, and Celia in the dressing area and told them to meet me downstairs. I knew Dmitri would be down there, waiting for Anya. If the other girls walked home with us (even part of the way) I would not feel like such an outsider with Anya and her new best friend, Dmitri. It made me so angry when they whispered secrets to each other on the way to and from work each day. Well, today I would just ignore them and talk with my friends as we walked along.

I picked up my coat and hurried to get in line, so I could enter the stairway and leave the eighth floor. As I stood there behind several other girls who were already in line, I noticed Eva Harris acting kind of strange. She was the sister of one of the owners of the company. She seemed upset. She raced over to Mr. Bernstein, the production manager, and frantically pointed across the room.

I smelled smoke.

I looked over in the direction where Miss Harris was pointing.

Flames were leaping up from one of the bins under a table in the center of the room.

Small fires often started at the Triangle Shirtwaist Company so I did not get excited about this one. Now, several of the men who were tailors on our floor were dousing the flames with water from the metal buckets that lined the walls of the room, as they usually did when small fires broke out. But today that only seemed to feed the fire. Max Rother was standing there with the other tailors.

Surely Mr. Rother can put out the fire.

Surprisingly, all Mr. Rother did was watch the other men. He must have been paralyzed with fear, as so many other people appeared to be, now that the fire was spreading.

Mr. Bernstein rushed to help the tailors, but the fire kept getting larger and larger, feeding on scraps of fabric in the room, so he and another man dragged in a water hose. It was rotted in places, and water would not flow through it, so they quickly tossed the hose aside.

Girls were screaming as they pushed past me to get to the stairway door as I stood there wondering which way to turn. The girls were so excited they forgot that the door opened inward, so they could not open it.

"Back up!" yelled one of the girls, "or we'll never get this door open!"

After much pushing and shoving, the girls backed away from the door enough to get it open. When they did, they rushed out and down the stairs as fast as they could go.

I knew I had to get up to the ninth floor and find Anya.

But then I realized that I had dropped my coat in all the excitement.

My pay envelope. I left it in my coat pocket. I must find my coat.

Everything was happening so fast. I was trapped in the middle of a crowd of girls, so all I could do was try to move forward with the crowd. I watched as girls on the Washington Place side of the room tried to open the door to the stairway. But, as usual, it would not open. The only way we were ever allowed to go out of the factory in the evenings was through the Greene Street side. When the girls realized they would not be able to open the doors, many of them moved to the passenger elevators on the Washington Place side. But the elevators were not on our floor.

A few seconds later, a passenger elevator passed by on its way down from the ninth or tenth floor. Finally, the other passenger elevator arrived and girls crowded into it. Each small elevator was designed to carry no more than fifteen people at a time, so I held my breath as I saw dozens of people pack into it. I prayed it would make its way down to the ground floor safely. As it started down, several frightened girls leaped onto the top of the elevator car. Others wrapped their hands in fabric, then grabbed the rough cables at the top of the elevator car to slide down onto it. With the weight of so many people, I was surprised the cable wires did not snap in two, right then and there. But the car kept lowering. Finally, the other elevator car arrived and more girls packed into it.

The room grew smokier and hotter by the minute. Hysterical girls and young women screamed and charged toward the stairway doors on both sides of the room, even though they could not get out on the Washington Place side. When they figured that out, many of them on the Washington Place side doused themselves with water from some of the metal buckets, then climbed onto the tables to leap through the fire to make their way to the stairs on the Greene Street side of the building. In some cases, the girls' hair or dresses caught fire, but they kept right on running, not bothering to put out the flames.

I glanced up to see the flimsy paper patterns hanging from wires burn quickly across the length of the room and fall over the heads of some of the girls who were still seated at their machines, paralyzed by fear. The smell of burning sewing machine oil and the dyes of fabrics filled the air.

I gave up all thoughts of trying to find my coat with my pay envelope. I needed to get to the stairway and go upstairs to find Anya.

Mr. Rother ran for the stairs on the Greene Street side of the building. I tried to push my way through the crowd of girls, but I noticed something that made me sick to my stomach.

It was Mary. The always bright and cheerful, Mary. Only, for once she did not appear bright and cheerful. She seemed terrified and unable to decide what to do.

She was still on the Washington Place side. And neither of the elevators had come back up again.

I pushed my way to a table and scrambled over it, trying to get to Mary. But the fire was out of control now and was racing toward me. I backed up as the flames grew closer and I could feel the heat.

I realized there was no way Mary could reach the stairway door on the Greene Street side of the building— the only stairway that was unlocked.

"Get out of here, Mary!" I shouted. "Use the elevators!"

I did not know if she heard me. There was so much screaming and crying in the room. Plus, the windows suddenly shattered as if they had been hit with a baseball bat. They made a loud popping sound, and the fire itself was so strong by now it roared like a freight train.

I cannot do anything for Mary. I just hope one of the elevators comes back up for her and the others. Now I must find Anya!

I turned and headed for the stairway on the Greene Street side.

Girls were crushing up against one another, trying to squeeze through the doorway to the stairs. I finally managed to get to the stairway. But it was almost impossible to get up the stairs to the ninth floor because I was moved along in a sea of girls charging downstairs to the street below. Plus, the stairway was filling with smoke.

Still, I fought my way back up.

Now the smoke in the stairwell was so thick and black, I could not see much of anything. I held my scarf to my face to block out some of the smoke.

All at once, a girl appeared on the stairs in front of me. She had obviously come down from one of the higher floors.

"Have you seen Anya Borchek?" I asked. "She's an operator on the ninth floor."

The girl looked puzzled. She must not have realized the building was on fire until she started to walk down the stairs.

Maybe none of the girls on the ninth or tenth floor knows what's happening until they get out into the stairway. They're probably all just standing around up there talking and laughing, without a care in the world.

"Have you seen my sister Anya?" I asked her again.

"Anya who?" she finally asked, then she coughed and covered her face with her scarf.

"Anya Borchek," I repeated. "She works on the ninth floor."

The girl shook her head. "No, I don't know her, but . . . "

The girl did not finish her sentence, she was choking on the smoke. She took off down the stairs as if she suddenly realized the building was on fire and she knew she should get out quickly.

I passed a few more girls coming down the stairs.

"There's a fire on the eighth floor!" I yelled to them. "Get out of the building!"

The girls quickly pushed past me and I finally made my way to the doorway of the ninth floor.

Until I got out of the stairway, I could not see much of anything but smoke. I coughed and covered my face with my scarf to take a breath, then entered the ninth floor.

Right away I recognized one of the girls who worked on this floor. Her name was Bessie Gabrilowich. She and another girl were dancing. I heard singing coming from the dressing room on the Washington Place side of the building.

It's probably the girls who had the cake earlier to celebrate someone's engagement.

A girl came out of the dressing room. I knew her, too. She was Rose Glantz and she was still singing. I even recognized the song, "Every Little Movement Has a Meaning All Its Own."

Other girls filed out of the dressing room behind her. They were singing as well. Some were giggling.

Good. The fire has not spread to this floor yet. I should have time to find Anya.

But before I could move, flames shot up through the floor ahead of me, engulfing some of the poor girls who still sat bent over at their sewing machines.

Oh, my God. It was so fast . . . they don't even know what happened to them.

Flames broke the windows. As the windows exploded, the songs and laughter turned to hysterical screams, and girls raced off in all directions. Bessie headed back to the dressing room, but I heard a foreman shout to her in Yiddish, "Bessie, save yourself." At that, Bessie turned around, covered her face with her purse, and ran to the stairway.

The girls were completely panicked as the flames raced through the room.

I scanned the room, trying to locate Anya. But the smoke was getting thick, and flames were lapping up everywhere. Girls climbed over the tables from the Washington Place side, trying to get to the stairway on the Greene Street side. Other girls pushed themselves up against the doorway on the Washington Street side, then screamed and beat their fists against the door when it would not open. But the door must have become too hot because they soon stopped.

When Rose seemed to realize that the Washington Place stairway door would not open, and there was no chance at the passenger elevators, I saw her wrap her scarf around her head, then run to the freight elevator side. She ran right through the doorway to the Greene Street stairs. I kept watching her.

Surely, she'll make it out alive. Hurry, Rose!

I turned back to the room and saw the most terrifying thing of all. The hysterical girls pushed one another toward the windows. The girls in the back were so panicked that they pushed the girls ahead of them right up to the windows, so they were shoved outside to the ground below. Other girls stepped out onto the ledge, ready to make the jump intentionally. Their hair, and in some cases their clothing, was on fire. The girls hesitated at the window for just a moment, then a few of them held hands and jumped, their clothes and hair ablaze. I could only hope that firemen were downstairs on the street, holding safety nets so the girls would be rescued.

"Anya! Anya!" I yelled, but my screams were soon cut off by a hacking cough.

The smoke was choking me. I struggled to take a breath.

I could not stop coughing. My head felt very, very hot and I smelled something strange, like singed feathers.

I looked up to see a bucket of cold water being thrown in my face.

I blinked, then shivered as the water soaked my clothes and my entire body.

"Your hair was on fire, miss," said a man's voice. "And we'll both be burned alive if we don't get out of here right now."

The man stepped toward me and pulled on my sleeve, as if he wanted to drag me out of the room, back to the stairway.

"No! No!" I screamed. "My sister . . . my sister is in here. I have to save my sister."

I tried to pull free of the man. Then I punched him with my fists before he gave up and ran away. I turned to run back into the room, but I felt someone wrap their arms around me from behind and pick me up to carry me down the stairs.

I fainted before I could see who it was.

chapter five

Amid the Ashes

hen I came to, I was headed down the stairs in someone's arms. I glanced up and caught a glimpse of the person's face through the smoke.

"Dmitri . . . where is Anya?" I whispered, then I drifted off again.

It must have been just a few moments later when fresh air and sunlight caused me to regain consciousness. We were now outside on the sidewalk.

What is going on? Why do I hear horses and people screaming?

Dmitri set me down on a blanket just as a woman spread it out on the sidewalk for him. Then he took off.

Where is he going? Why is he leaving me? Where am I? Wait . . . Dmitri!

I was too weak from inhaling so much smoke to actually call out to Dmitri. I lay on the blanket and coughed so hard I was afraid my insides were going to come up.

The woman leaned down beside me. "Are you injured, miss? Do you need to be taken to a hospital?"

When I didn't answer her, she called out to two men. They charged over and lifted me in their arms and transported me to a building across the street. The woman followed us into the lobby on the ground floor of the building. I noticed other people lying on the floor there. Some of them were moaning or sobbing.

"You'll be safer here, miss," said one of the men, then both of them ran back in the direction of the Asch building.

"Are you sure you're not injured?" asked the woman again. She examined my arms and legs. "You don't seem to have any burns or cuts. Here, try to sip some water." She held a cup to my lips.

I had stopped coughing and I tried to sit up to take a sip of the water, but the room was spinning. "I'm all right," I said. "I just need to rest for a few minutes."

The woman wiped my face with a piece of cloth, probably a handkerchief, and smoothed back my hair.

"You poor child," she said, "You've been through a terrible ordeal. But you're safe now. Just rest. I'll come back to you in a few minutes. I must check on the others."

I lay there trying to breathe, but every breath was painful because so much smoke had entered my lungs. Memories came flooding back to me.

Fire! The building was on fire! I have to find Anya! Where is Anya?

I sat up slowly and looked around at the girls and young women lying on the floor all around me. A small girl sat huddled over another girl who was stretched out on the floor. Both of their faces were so dirty from the fire that I did not recognize them until the one lying down began to cry. "Oh, Minnie. Where are the other girls? Did our friends escape?"

I struggled to my feet. "Celia! Minnie!" I called out to them as I managed to make my way over to their corner.

Celia did not try to sit or stand. I noticed her foot was bloody and mangled. She looked up at me. "Oh, thank God, Galena . . . you are safe!" She reached up to take my hands in hers. I bent down and hugged her. Minnie hugged me, too, then she started to cry softly. Tears streaked her blackened face, making white lines from her eyes to her chin.

"What happened?" I asked. "How did you escape?"

"My foot was caught in the cage of the elevator when all the other girls pushed me into it," said Celia. "The door to the staircase wouldn't open. We pushed to the passenger elevators. Everybody was pushing and screaming. When the car stopped at our floor the crowd pushed me into it. I began to scream for my sister. I had lost her, I had lost my sister."

Minnie cuddled up beside Celia and hugged her. "But I'm here now," she said to her.

I smoothed Celia's hair, and reassured her, "Yes, Minnie is here now, Celia. You have not lost her."

"I fainted in the elevator," said Celia. "It was so crowded that I couldn't have fallen to the floor. We were packed in there like pencils in a box. I could barely breathe with all the girls jammed up against me on all sides. When I came to, Minnie was here, bending over me. It was the most beautiful sight I had ever seen."

I brushed back my own tears now as I thought of Anya.

"I have to go, Celia. I have to find my own sister."

Celia gasped. "Oh, Galena. Anya did not escape with you?"

I shook my head.

"What about Mary? And Rebecca? Have you seen either of them?" asked Minnie.

"No," I whispered. "I haven't seen Rebecca at all since lunch. The last time I saw Mary she was standing on the Washington Place side. I yelled at her to take the elevator. Didn't you see her there, Celia?"

Celia closed her eyes. "It was all a blur of girls pushing and shoving and all that smoke. I'm sorry, Galena. I didn't see her . . . I didn't see her."

She started to sob. I comforted her for a few moments, then excused myself and went to the front window to look out at all the commotion in the street. People were racing everywhere. Some were screaming, others were crying. Firemen were spraying water from hoses, trying to put the fire out, but the water wouldn't reach any higher than the sixth floor of the building so it was completely useless.

Big bundles of fabric were all over the sidewalk on the other side of the street and also on the street itself. I walked outside so I could see things more closely.

Oh, my God . . . those are not bundles of fabric!

They were bodies of the girls who had jumped or been pushed out the windows.

The firemen had not been there to catch them.

I started to cry.

"Here! Jump here! We'll save you! We'll save you!" Four men were holding a horse blanket. They stretched it out flat to catch a group of girls perched on the window ledge above.

Wait! Jump one at a time! The blanket is not strong enough to hold all of you at once.

But the girls all jumped together. They were too terrified to each take a turn.

The blanket ripped apart like paper when the girls struck it.

The girls smashed to the street.

I turned my face away from the sight. I thought I would be sick, but then I could not help myself. I looked back at the street. The dead girls lay in a heap, not moving. The men stood horrified. Two of them were still clutching pieces of the blanket in a daze.

Firemen held up nets to catch some of the other girls. But, again, too many jumped at once, and they broke through the net and were killed.

There must have been thousands of people standing on the sidewalks now, looking on, and screaming in horror at the girls who were trapped on the ninth floor of the building and were leaning out the windows.

I looked up again. Smoked poured out of all three top floors of the Asch building and the sky was turning black. When I had been upstairs on the ninth floor, I had witnessed girls being shoved through the windows by the hysterical crowd. But now, more and more of the girls were jumping deliberately. It was either jump to their deaths or be burned alive. No wonder so many of them chose to jump.

A young couple stood on the ledge. They kissed, then leaped into the air.

Another girl stood holding a fire bucket. She jumped, too, still holding tightly to the useless pail.

Another young woman tossed her purse, her hat, and finally herself to the street.

One familiar-looking girl was making her way outside the window now to the ledge. Her clothing was filthy from the smoke and the ashes floating through the air in the building, and part of the skirt of her dress was gone. It must have been burned or ripped away. I could not tell the color of her garments. But I could tell she wasn't wearing a shirtwaist like so many of the other young girls.

Oh, no! Rebecca . . .

I studied the girl more closely.

That is Rebecca . . . and her hair is starting to catch on fire.

All at once, Rebecca screamed and leaped from the window. Her dress ballooned out away from her like an umbrella opening, and her hair was a mass of flames as she plunged toward the ground.

I screamed again. "No! Rebecca, no!" I turned away before she hit the ground. But then I had a terrifying thought.

Is Anya with her? Will Anya appear at the window next?

I did not take my eyes off the ninth-floor windows for several minutes. I kept expecting Anya to be among the young girls who appeared on the window ledge and then jumped, but I never saw her.

After witnessing so many young girls jump to their deaths, I fell to my knees, still sobbing. Finally, so many people shoved against me, I was forced to get up or be trampled by the crowd.

I heard the clanging of fire bells.

More fire wagons and ambulances arrived. By this time, they were having trouble getting up the street to the burning building. The roadway and sidewalks were littered with piles of dead bodies. Water from the fire hoses mixed with the blood of those dead on the ground. It flowed down the street. The smell of blood and death were very strong. The horses pulling the fire wagons and ambulances looked scared. Many of them reared back and refused to go any closer to the building.

In my heart I knew there probably was not anything I could do to save Anya if she were still inside the Asch building. But I ran back to the Greene Street doors to try. A group of firemen was there. They were working to get girls out who were trapped on top of the elevator cars or still on the stairs.

"You can't go in there, miss," said one of the firemen. He held a hatchet in his hands and used it to bar the doorway so I could not get through.

"But my sister . . . I have to find my sister," I shouted at him.

"It's too late for anyone up there," he said. "It's so hot and smoky the firemen can't even make it back up the stairs."

I felt someone's arms on my shoulders. I turned around to face one of the male cutters from my floor.

"Come, little one," he said gently. "If your sister is safe, someone will find her. There is nothing you can do here."

The man led me away from the building with his arms around my shoulders as I sobbed uncontrollably.

chapter six

We Keep Up Hope

O nce we were away from the building and I had managed to stop crying, I looked up to see Dmitri rushing toward us from the building across the street, where he had left me just a short time ago, although it seemed like hours had passed since then.

Dmitri thanked the man for helping me and told him he would take care of me now. When the man had walked away, Dmitri looked down at me. "What are you doing, Galena? I told you I would be back for you. You were safe across the street. Why did you come back here?"

Why are you telling me what I should do? Why must you always be so bossy? I do not need your help. I can take care of myself.

"I wanted to look for Anya." I told him. "Did you find her? Have you seen Anya?"

I knew she would be with him now if he had found her, so since I did not see her, I started to cry again.

Surprisingly, Dmitri put his arms around me. There were tears in his eyes, too, but I could tell he was trying to be strong and reassuring. "Don't give up hope yet, Galena. She might have escaped. We just need to continue searching for her."

I wiped my tears away with the hem of my dress. "Where do we start?" I asked. "Where do we look for her?"

Dmitri took my hand. "Come with me."

I followed him as he led me through the crowd.

Smoke still poured out from the top three floors of the Asch building and the entire sky was dark now.

People were coming from all directions to see what was happening.

"Why are we leaving?" I asked. "Where are we going?"

"To the hospital," said Dmitri. "Anya doesn't seem to be among those who jumped, and I talked to a man named Mr. Morris Lewine a few minutes ago. He is one of the bookkeepers for the Triangle Shirtwaist Company. He said he was working on the tenth floor when the fire started. He made his way to the roof. Two girls followed him. He was able to find a ladder and make his way with one of the girls to the roof of an adjoining building. That girl might have been Anya. She might have gone up to the tenth floor if she couldn't make her way down the stairs because the fire had already spread so quickly."

I tried to make sense of what Dmitri was saying.

"But you just said there were two girls with this man . . . this Mr. Lewine. What happened to the other girl?"

Dmitri shrugged. "Mr. Lewine did not know."

I swallowed a lump in my throat.

Please, God . . . let Anya be the girl who escaped with Mr. Lewine.

As we made our way through the crowd, I heard several young men explaining to others how they had rescued several of the Triangle workers. Dmitri heard them, too.

"Excuse me, sirs," said Dmitri. He removed his cap as he approached the young men. "Could you describe the people you rescued?"

The young men looked at one another and shook their heads.

"Not really," said one of the men. "They were all fairly young and most of them were women and girls. That is all I can tell you."

Dmitri must have looked confused because another of the young men said, "We are law students at New York University, which adjoins the Asch building. We were able to help them escape from the burning building by crossing over the roof. After the women got to our building they couldn't wait to get down to the ground floor and run outside. They were frantic. Just terrified. A few of them had been burned or cut and needed medical attention. You might check the hospitals."

"Thank you," said Dmitri. He bowed slightly at the young men, then he put his cap back on.

Frightened relatives were searching for their loved ones everywhere now. I could hear the pain and fear in their voices as they passed by.

"I told her to find work in a union shop," said a young woman clutching a shawl around her shoulders.

"She would have been long gone from the building before this fire ever started today if this had been a union shop," said another.

I noticed an older man and woman searching among the bodies heaped on the sidewalk. They were probably the parents of some poor girl lost in the fire.

I suddenly thought of Mama and Papa.

Do they even know about the fire?

Then I had a much happier thought.

"Do you think Anya went home?" I asked Dmitri. "She might be there right now, and quite frantic that she can't find me." I turned around to head for our apartment. "I'm going home."

For once, Dmitri did not try to convince me that he knew best. He simply followed me. We ran down the sidewalk. We had gone about fifteen blocks when I spotted Mama and Papa on the sidewalk about half a block ahead of us. Evidently, they had heard about the fire and were on their way to the Asch building.

I raced to them and collapsed in Mama's arms.

She smothered me with kisses . . . and tears.

"Galena! My precious child, you are safe," she said in Yiddish as she rocked me back and forth in her arms.

Papa rushed to Dmitri and put a hand on his shoulder. "We heard about the fire. Everyone has heard about it by now. Where is Anya?"

Dmitri removed his cap. "We don't know, sir," he said. "We were on our way to your apartment to see if she had gone home to look for Galena."

Mama looked at him. "She has not been home."

"I've searched the streets around the Asch building for her," Dmitri said. "I did not find Anya there."

I pulled away from Mama. "But some nice men from the university said they rescued several young women from the fire. Anya might be one of them."

Dmitri nodded. "And some of those who were rescued were taken to the hospital, so that is where I will look now."

"I will go with you," said Papa. "Mama, you and Galena go home and wait there for Anya."

Mama took my hand. "Of course," she said. "Come, Galena."

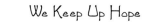

I jerked my hand away from her. "No! I want to go with Dmitri! I must search for Anya! It is my duty! I'm the one who left the building without her." I started to sob.

Mama put her arms around me again, then she said softly, "Dmitri and Papa can search for Anya. I can't go home alone, Galena. I will need someone to stay with me."

She was right, of course. She could not go home alone at a time like this. Yet I realized she must have known how I felt about leaving Anya in the building. Mama felt responsible for her own sister's death so many years ago. And now, if Anya had died, I would feel responsible since I had left the building without her. If there was something I could do to save Anya—anything I could do—then surely Mama would allow me to do it.

"I don't want you to be alone at a time such as this, Mama. But I must go search for Anya." I looked at her pleadingly. "Perhaps Papa could stay with you."

Mama did not speak. She and Papa stared at each other. After a few moments, Papa patted my back. "Then go, Galena. Go with Dmitri and find your sister."

I pulled myself away from Mama and gave Papa a hug.

Dmitri took my hand. "We'll be back as soon as we find Anya," he assured Mama and Papa.

chapter seven

The Search for Anya

D mitri decided we would go back to the Asch building to see if Anya had shown up there. If we still did not find her, we would go to St. Vincent's Hospital where many of the injured had most likely been taken since it was one of the hospitals closest to the fire.

As we approached the Asch Building, the street and sidewalks were filled with even more onlookers, policemen, and firemen than before. We pushed our way through the crowd, searching for Anya. I called her name, over and over again. But no one answered.

I lost all sense of time, but we must have searched for hours when Dmitri finally decided we had searched there long enough.

A pile of bodies lay on the sidewalk a few yards from us. The policemen and firemen started to remove the

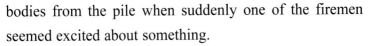

bodies from the pile when suddenly one of the firemen seemed excited about something.

"There's a girl here who's still breathing," he shouted. "Quick, get her to the ambulance!"

The fireman stayed with her, while another man ran to a nearby ambulance. A few moments later, he and another man returned carrying a stretcher. The fireman who had remained with the girl on the sidewalk looked up at them and shook his head. "It's too late," he said. "She's gone now."

I noticed a policeman going around to the dead bodies on the street and fastening a tag to the wrist of each one, then he wrote something on the tag with a pencil.

"What's he doing?" I asked Dmitri.

Dmitri took my hand in his and looked at me sadly. "He's putting tags on the bodies to help identify them."

"But he couldn't possibly know all their names," I said not fully understanding what was going on.

"No, he doesn't know their names. He is just giving each body a number right now so the police have some way of identifying each of them."

Tears rolled down my cheeks, but I felt numb and too tired to sob any longer. Dmitri walked off to question other people he recognized in the crowd.

So many people were approaching the fire scene from Washington Square now that a line of policemen tried to hold back the crowd to give the firemen room to remove the bodies from the sidewalks and the street.

The fireman stretched out a piece of red canvas on the sidewalk across the street from the Asch building on the Greene Street side. One by one, bodies were lifted and placed on the canvas.

A line of ambulances and patrol wagons drove up to the building. They brought dozens upon dozens of plain pine wooden caskets. A body was placed in each casket, then the caskets were loaded into an ambulance or patrol wagon and taken away.

I noticed a policeman picking up personal belongings from the street. There were combs, purses, shoes, hats—all items that had belonged to the girls who jumped to their deaths.

I heard someone in the crowd say that policemen at the Mercer Street Police Station were giving out information about the dead and the injured.

"Shouldn't we go there first?" I asked Dmitri.

But he shook his head and said, "We're going to the hospital first."

Apparently, he was not ready to give up hope yet of Anya being found alive. For once I agreed with him.

I'm not ready to give up hope yet either, Dmitri.

As daylight faded, searchlights from two fire trucks were used to light up the outside of the Asch building.

They cast an eerie glow against the stone structure. And, oddly enough, a fire alarm continued to ring from somewhere in the building. I had not noticed it before. Now it seemed like a sad, awful joke.

A fireman on the roof lowered a hook to the ninth-floor window. The crowd below seemed fascinated. Several other firemen pulled the hook inside. A few minutes later the hook swung out of the window again. This time a wrapped bundle was attached to it. It was lowered to the ground as firemen in the windows on each floor kept it from hitting against the building on its way down.

I stood there in a daze, as fascinated and horrified as everyone else, watching bundle after bundle lowered from the ninth floor. Finally Dmitri grabbed my hand and pulled me along.

"But Anya might be up there," I told him, pointing to the window where a wrapped bundle was on its way down to the street.

He let go of my hand, took off his cap, and wiped his sweaty forehead. "If she is, then they'll probably take her to the hospital morgue. Let's go."

St. Vincent's Hospital was not very far away. It did not take us long to walk there. Other people were headed there, too, so we followed them.

When we got to the hospital, a swarm of other people who had come searching for lost loved ones was already there.

Hospital workers had lists of some of the injured who were conscious and able to identify themselves. The more seriously injured had not all been identified.

Dmitri led me to a bench in the waiting room. "Sit here. I will be back in a few minutes," he said.

I saw him approach a group of nurses. They shook their heads as he obviously asked them questions. A few moments later, one of the nurses led him out of the room and he followed her down the hall.

As I sat waiting for him, I must have laid down because the next thing I knew he was gently shaking me awake.

"Wake up, Galena," he said. "Anya is not here."

"Where are we going now?" I asked him as we exited St. Vincent's.

"To another hospital," he said, "to Bellevue."

Bellevue Hospital was many blocks away. I was exhausted yet filled with nervous energy. I kept walking, making my way through the hundreds of people on the sidewalk. Dmitri and I were not the only ones headed to Bellevue. It felt as if everyone in the city was searching for a missing loved one.

When we finally got to Bellevue, the scene was much the same as it had been at St. Vincent's. People were everywhere. Hospital workers were trying to organize the chaos.

I waited for Dmitri again while he talked to workers there. I had expected to see stretchers bringing in those injured in the fire, but I did not see any injured people come in. Instead, ambulances came and went, bringing bundles in blankets each time they returned. Eventually, the ambulances stopped delivering the bundles. I took that as good news.

All the dead have been collected now. How many could there have been? Maybe twenty-five or so?

I tried to tell myself that most of the girls had escaped unharmed. But I knew in my heart that it was unlikely. I could still picture all those girls standing on the ledges of the ninth-floor windows. I had no idea how many I had seen.

Dmitri came striding toward me. "Anya's not here either," he told me. "Let's go."

"Where are we going now?" I asked. "To another hospital?"

"Just walk," said Dmitri. "You'll find out soon enough."

I trailed along behind him, trying to keep up. He was walking so quickly, though. It was difficult. But I did not want to ask him to slow down.

When we came to a barricade at First Avenue and Twenty-sixth Street, I knew we were not headed to another hospital. A huge crowd had gathered behind the barricade. Dmitri pulled me by the hand behind him as he pushed his way to the front of the crowd.

I saw a police wagon stop and unload more bundles. I knew what was inside each one.

Everyone knows what is inside those blankets.

The policemen tried to keep the crowd contained behind the barricade. But frantic relatives of the victims broke through it whenever a new group of bundles was delivered.

Some pulled the blankets from the bundles, revealing the body underneath.

As someone recognized a loved one, they released eerie wails of sadness, anger, and despair. They were the saddest sounds I had ever heard. Like wild animals crying out in intense pain. Some of the women even fainted when they saw a dead person they recognized.

Dmitri tried to keep me from seeing the bodies.

"Stay back, Galena," he told me. "You don't need to see any of this. If Anya is here, I will find her."

I backed away from the crowd and sat down on the ground.

This cannot be happening. I must be having a terrible, terrible nightmare. Yes, that's it. It's all just a horrible, horrible dream . . .

But when I looked up, I knew it was real.

The nightmare was real.

A policeman made some sort of announcement. I could not hear what he said. But the crowd moved quickly, forming two lines. I noticed Dmitri had managed to position himself at the head of one of the lines.

I felt useless, just sitting there on the ground, so I joined Dmitri.

"What's going on?" I asked him. "What is this place? It is not a hospital."

"No," agreed Dmitri. "It is not a hospital. It is a temporary morgue."

Dmitri took my hands in his. "They will let us in to identify bodies at midnight. Until then, we wait."

I knew then that whether or not Dmitri and I liked it, all hope of finding Anya alive was gone.

We stood in line for what seemed like days. Periodically, a policeman would announce some girl's name from a pay envelope found on one of the bodies or say he had a piece of jewelry with certain initials on it. He would ask if anyone in the crowd was searching for someone by that name or those initials. Many times a woman or man would come to the front of the line and follow the policeman when an announcement like this was made. Then we would hear a loud scream or wail in the background as the person recognized their loved one among the dead.

At one point, the policeman asked, "Is anyone here looking for Rebecca Feicisch or Feibish?" He seemed confused about her last name.

No one came forward. Dmitri and I stared at each other. I started to take a step forward, but Dmitri stopped me. He knew Rebecca, and he would be able to identify her, because she often walked to work with us in the mornings.

"I am!" he said, raising his hand so the policeman could spot him. "I'm looking for Rebecca."

The policeman led Dmitri back to identify Rebecca's body.

I said a prayer for Rebecca as I waited for Dmitri to return.

When he did come back, he did not say anything. He looked at me and nodded to indicate the body was indeed Rebecca's.

I knew that was Rebecca I saw jumping from the building today. Oh, Rebecca, I'm so sorry . . .

Dmitri stroked my hair as I cried softly for Rebecca.

At midnight, just as the policeman had said, they began letting people in to identify the bodies and the lines started moving. Only a few at a time were allowed in, though, so the lines moved slowly. Since we were at the front of the line, we were the first to go in. I was thankful for that. I was tired of waiting. But then Dmitri said, "Stay here, Galena. This will not be pleasant. If Anya is here, it may be best if you did not have to see her."

From my position at the front of the line, I had already glimpsed some of the bodies lined up in coffins, just beyond the barricade. They were not disfigured or burned too badly, although many had died with a look of horror on their faces, so it was not pleasant to see them.

I would rather remember Anya when she was alive and happy—not like these girls.

"Yes, I will stay here," I whispered to Dmitri.

As he entered the morgue, I silently prayed that he would not find Anya there.

"Come sit down, miss," said a policeman. He led me to a wooden bench.

I waited for Dmitri and prayed for all those around me who screamed out in anguish as they identified a loved one.

After what seemed like hours, Dmitri reappeared.

I walked over to him, but I could not bring myself to ask him if he had found Anya.

He did not seem to be able to speak either. He led me back to the bench and we sat down.

Dmitri reached for my hands and opened them. Then he slipped something inside them.

I knew what it was even before I looked down at it.

Anya's locket. Her treasured locket that she always wears around her neck. She never takes it off. She didn't lose it or sell it. Oh, how I almost wish she had now.

I looked down at the locket in my hands. The clasp and chain were still in perfect condition, so the locket had not come undone and fallen away from Anya's neck. Someone must have just removed it when Dmitri identified her body.

Dmitri and I were both crying now. There was no reason to be strong and hopeful any longer.

Anya is gone. I have lost my sister forever! Oh, Anya . . . my beloved, Anya!

Dmitri held me in his arms and we wept together for a long time.

Finally, neither of us had any tears left. We sat there quietly until I fell asleep from exhaustion.

I awoke to find myself lying on the bench, with my head resting on Dmitri's jacket. He had taken it off and made a pillow out of it for me. I must have just moved my head into a different position, though, because I felt

something hard and lumpy in one of the pockets and was so uncomfortable I woke.

Dmitri still sat on the bench beside me.

"Ah . . . you're awake," he said. "Are you feeling rested enough to walk home now?"

I sat up and nodded. For a moment, I had forgotten where we were. "That is not a very soft pillow." I patted the jacket pocket.

Dmitri's face reddened and he jerked the jacket away from me. "Oh, there must be a pencil in that pocket. But no matter. We should be leaving now anyway." He stood up and reached for my hand. "Come . . . we must give your mama and papa the sad news."

Now I remembered.

The fire . . . Anya is gone . . . I no longer have a sister . . . and now we must go home to let Mama and Papa know.

chapter eight

I Learn More of the Fire

I dreaded the thought of returning home and giving Mama and Papa the terrible news. It would break their hearts. Mama had already experienced so much sadness in her life. First, losing her sister and feeling responsible for her death, then losing her father, and then leaving her own mother behind in Russia. How would Mama live with the news that her older daughter had died in a tragic fire? The daughter she had taken halfway around the world in the hopes of giving her a safer, less violent life.

Dmitri and I walked along in silence. I guess neither of us knew what to say. But when we were at the end of our block, Dmitri stopped and turned to me.

"Let me speak to your mama and papa," he said. "The news will be easier to take coming from me."

I nodded in agreement.

I do not think I could get any words out of my mouth to tell them something that will bring them such sadness. I'm so sad myself. For once, I am glad to have you take over, Dmitri.

When we got to my apartment building, Dmitri pulled open the door for me. We trudged up the stairs to my family's third-story apartment. Mama must have seen us out the window because when Papa opened the door, we found Mama sitting at the table, sobbing into a handkerchief.

"The news is not good then?" asked Papa, studying Dmitri's face.

Dmitri shook his head.

I ran to Mama and she wrapped her arms around me.

"Sit down, my son," said Papa. "Were you able to identify her? I mean . . . you know for certain it was Anya."

Dmitri slowly nodded and sat down at the table across from Papa. I pulled away from Mama and reached for Papa's hand. I turned it over, then I placed Anya's locket in his palm.

"This is how we know for certain that it was Anya, Papa," I said.

Tears ran down Papa's cheeks as he recognized the locket.

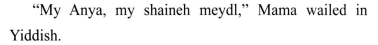

"My Anya, my shaineh meydl," Mama wailed in Yiddish.

Now I'm the only shaineh meydl you have left, Mama.

"We should collect the body," said Papa. "And arrange for burial."

He put the locket back in my hands and got up from the table.

I knew we would follow the traditional Jewish customs for burial or at least some of them. That meant Anya would be buried as soon as possible and, following the burial, we would "sit shivah" for seven days. But right now, it was the middle of the night and I was exhausted. I wanted to sleep because it was the only way to get away from the horrible truth. In my dreams, Anya would still be alive.

Mama tucked me into bed and I closed my eyes. But my mind was racing, reliving the horrible fire and that terrible moment when Dmitri had placed Anya's treasured locket in my hands. I unclasped the locket and placed it around my own neck now.

I will wear it always, Anya, just as you did. You and Bubbie will be with me always.

I started to drift off several times, but each time I would realize my sister was gone forever, and I would be wide-awake again.

Yet finally . . . I slept.

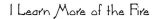

The next few days were a blur of activity. Doorways throughout the Lower East Side were decorated with flowers, indicating someone who lived there had been lost in the fire. New York City became a city of death, with funeral processions for victims of the Triangle fire each day.

Mama said that arrangements had been made with the Workmen's Circle (a society that provided death benefits for Jewish workers) for the Jewish victims of the fire to be buried at Mount Zion Cemetery. Many of the Jewish girls were buried there on the same day.

Even though Anya was not a member of the union, a woman from the Women's Trade Union League came to our home, to see if we needed money for anything or help making the funeral arrangements. I am not sure what Mama told her. The woman did not stay at our apartment long.

We buried Anya on Monday. I do not remember much about it, though. I think I was numb during the entire thing since I was trying to convince myself that none of it was truly happening. I remember seeing Dmitri. His eyes were red with dark circles beneath them.

As we watched Anya's plain pine coffin resting in the grave that day, I opened the gold locket and stared at the photo of Mama, Papa, Anya, and me.

You will always be with me, Anya. Now I will say good-bye to your picture each morning as I leave for work.

I also remember that immediately following the burial, we returned to our apartment to receive visitors and sit shivah, just as we had done two years earlier in Russia when my grandfather had died. But this time it was so much sadder. Grandfather had been an old man. He had lived a long life. Anya was just beginning her life. We should not be burying such a young woman.

Mama told me, "The hardest thing a mother might ever have to do is bury her child."

I thought about that a lot right before Anya's funeral.

So many young girls have been buried this week. So many engaged girls who were looking forward to a wonderful future with their husbands. Anya was one of those girls. We should not be burying Anya. We should not be burying my sister. And Mama should not be burying her child.

Now, as was the custom, a basin of water was placed outside our door, so those who attended the funeral could wash their hands before entering our apartment. This was to symbolize the separation of their duty of honoring Anya at the funeral with their new duty of comforting the bereaved at our home.

We removed our leather shoes and placed them by the door, and we put on cloth slippers as a sign that we were made humble by Anya's loss. Papa had taken our mattresses from their frames and set them on the floor because the grieving family needs to sit on low cushions for the seven days of shivah to show they have been "struck down by grief."

Mama, Papa, and I sat on the mattresses now, ready to receive *seudat havra'ah*, or the meal of consolation, which would be prepared by family friends. This meal consisted of "round" foods, which symbolized the circle of life. I choked down part of a boiled egg and some cooked lentils. I did not feel like eating, but Mama said we had to eat to show that life would go on.

Family friends sat in the wooden chairs in our kitchen area, quietly talking with Mama and Papa. I glanced around the apartment. The curtain that separated the sleeping area had been pulled back to give people more room to stand and walk about. The mirror above the washstand (the only mirror in our apartment) was covered with a black cloth to encourage us to reflect on our spirits now rather than our outward appearance. The shivah candle, or *ner daulk*, which means "bright light," burned on the dresser in the kitchen area to symbolize the spark that inhabits each of us. The door to our apartment would remain unlocked during shivah, so visitors could come in without the family having to do anything to let them enter. All regular activity stops for the bereaved family during

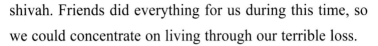

shivah. Friends did everything for us during this time, so we could concentrate on living through our terrible loss.

It seemed so unusual for Papa to be home during the day, and Mama to be sitting silently on a mattress rather than working furiously to assemble artificial flowers with other women from the neighborhood.

We did not even change clothes or bathe during shivah. After the first day, I was restless after the morning prayer or *shacharit*. Many of my friends from the Triangle Shirtwaist Company came by to offer their condolences. While Mama and Papa talked with their own friends, my friends whispered to me about the protests and marches that were going on throughout the city. For the first time, I felt like joining them.

Two of the girls who came to visit me during shivah were Rose Rosenfeld and Bessie Gabrilowich.

"Rose! Bessie!" I greeted them excitedly. "Thank you for being here. Let's go out to the fire escape where we can get some fresh air and talk."

We climbed through the window and Bessie and Rose sat down beside me on the iron railing.

"We're so, so sorry, Galena," said Rose. "Anya was a wonderful person."

I knew that Rose and Bessie had both worked on the ninth floor with Anya.

"Thank you," I said. I was more interested in their accounts of the fire since I already knew they had liked Anya. "Did you see Anya once the fire started?" I was anxious to learn anything I could about the last few moments of my sister's life.

Bessie shook her head. But Rose looked at me sheepishly.

"I saw her," said Rose. "When we heard about the fire, I decided to go up to the tenth floor where the owners and office workers were. I figured they would know what to do to save themselves. And they did. Mr. Harris and Mr. Blanck and others from the office were getting in the freight elevator, so I followed them. At first, I was surprised that we were headed up, not down. But then I realized we were going to the roof."

I suddenly remembered what the bookkeeper, Mr. Lewine, had told Dmitri about that day. "Was Anya with you? Did you see her there on the tenth floor?"

Rose nodded, but it seemed difficult for her to continue. Finally she did. "The elevator was full. Anya wasn't in the elevator. I saw her and another girl following another man just before we got in the elevator. After that . . . I never saw her again. I'm sorry, Galena."

I managed a weak smile. "Thank you, Rose. I think the man she was following was the bookkeeper, Mr. Lewine."

And Anya was the second girl following him. The girl he lost track of before they got out through the roof.

I looked at Bessie. "I saw you run down the stairs after the foreman yelled at you to save yourself," I told her.

Tears were streaming down Bessie's cheeks. "Yes, I did make it down the stairs. But my friend Dora did not. I went back to the Asch building the day after the fire. Bodies were lined up on the street outside the building so relatives could identify them. It was the most horrible sight I had ever seen. Dora was there with all those other dead girls. I fainted at the sight of them all."

Rose leaned forward, "She sure did. And some horrible newspaper photographer snapped her picture just as she collapsed! Can you believe anyone would be so insensitive?"

I didn't know what to think. I still found it difficult to believe anything about the last few days. It still felt like a horrible nightmare.

"I'm so sorry about Dora," I said to Bessie. "We have all lost many dear friends."

Bessie could not seem to speak. She just nodded.

"But there were some wonderful rescues that day, too," said Rose. "Firemen found Hyman Meshell in the basement of the building, nearly four hours after the fire started. He was in water up to his neck, just below the floor of an elevator car. Can you imagine that? His hands were

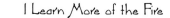

badly injured from sliding down the steel cable of the elevator. And his forearms and knuckles were full of glass splinters that he got when he beat through the glass door of the elevator shaft. But he was alive. He's in St. Vincent's Hospital right now."

"Oh, my goodness," I said. "The poor man. He must have been scared out of his mind. I'm so thankful he didn't escape the fire only to drown in the basement. How horrible!"

For several days, more girls from the Triangle Shirtwaist Company came by our apartment. Each one had her own story about the day of the fire. Minnie and her mother came by one morning. I found out that Celia's foot had been so badly injured in the elevator car that she was unable to walk and could not come with them. I was eager to talk to Minnie, to find out if she had heard from Mary.

Minnie took my hand in hers. "They found Mary's body, Galena," Minnie told me. "She was one of the girls who leaped onto the top of the elevator car. But so many leaped at once, Mary was crushed."

I gasped in horror. "Oh, no! I *told* Mary to use the elevator. I was the one who told her to get out that way! I caused her to jump to her death. Now I feel responsible for what happened to her!"

Minnie's mother put her arms around me. "There, there, Galena. It is not your fault. Nothing that happened that day is your fault. The elevator was the only way Mary could have escaped. And many girls did escape atop the elevator car. Mary was just not one of them. But that is not your fault."

Poor sweet Mary. She was always so bright and cheerful. Why did she have to die so young?

"Rebecca did not escape the fire either," said Minnie. "I'm not sure how she died, though, but we attended her funeral."

"I know she didn't escape," I said. "I saw her jump out the window from the ninth floor that day. Her hair was on fire. Dmitri identified her body at the morgue . . . " My voice trailed off and I was afraid I was going to cry uncontrollably.

"Do you know Pauline Grossman?" asked Minnie suddenly.

"I think so," I said, wiping a tear from my cheek. "Doesn't she, I mean . . . Didn't she work on the eighth floor?"

"I'm not sure, but I do know she got out of the building safely," said Minnie.

I smiled weakly. "That's wonderful," I said.

Minnie smiled, too, then she looked serious. "The union workers are outraged at what has happened," she said. "You should see the union halls. Black banners have been posted at each hall in mourning for the dead. And I hear a special meeting is going to be held in a few days."

Mama was busy talking with other friends and did not seem to notice us talking about union meetings, so I encouraged Minnie to continue.

"Are you going to the meeting, Minnie?" I asked.

She nodded. "Yes, and Celia would go, too, of course, if she were able. Mama is going with me, though."

Minnie's mother smiled and nodded. "Things must change," she said. "The union is the only way that will happen."

"Come to the meeting with us, Galena," urged Minnie. "The more girls who are there to support the union, the more powerful it will be."

"I don't know," I said. "Mama will be frightened for me if she knows a crowd will be there. She won't want me to go. Besides, I'm not so sure the union would do any good."

"That's what bosses like the owners of the Triangle Shirtwaist Company want you to think, Galena. They don't want things to change." Minnie leaned closer and whispered to me, "Anya knew that, and she was going to join the union. She told Celia she was ready to join, but first she wanted to convince your mama it was the right thing to do."

"I know," I whispered back to Minnie. "Mama and Anya were arguing about the union a few days before the fire. And that wasn't the first time they had argued about it either."

If Mama and I had listened to Anya, maybe she would still be alive. We would have been among those union workers who left the Asch building at noon on Saturday.

I tried to brush that thought from my mind. The fire had not been Mama's fault. I could not blame her for Anya's death. Still, I was beginning to think Mama was wrong about the union. Someone had to protect the workers from dangerous fires like this one. And the owners of the factories sure were not going to do it. Not until someone made them, that is.

On Thursday, an older woman I did not recognize came to our apartment. She sat with Mama, and the two of them whispered secretively, so I could not hear what they were saying. When the woman left, I moved over beside Mama and asked, "Who was that woman, Mama? I do not think I have ever seen her."

Mama wiped her eyes with a handkerchief. "She is the shadchen," Mama said in Yiddish. Then she looked at me and said in English, "the matchmaker."

I wondered if the matchmaker would return Mama's money now that she would no longer need her services.

chapter nine

Dmitri and the Union

Many times each day, I opened Anya's beautiful gold locket and admired the images of Bubbie and Anya inside. But even when the locket was closed, just wearing it made me feel closer to my sister. I rubbed the smooth oval piece of jewelry between my fingers as I thought about Anya and talked to her silently in my head. I remembered what Anya had said to me the last time I had asked her to open the locket so I could see the pictures inside: "They are only photographs in a locket. It's not like you will never see Mama and Papa again."

I wondered when Anya had opened the locket for the last time to admire the photographs.

If it was the day of the fire, she hadn't seen Mama and Papa ever again.

Occasionally, when too many people were crowded into our small apartment offering their condolences, I felt as if I could not breathe. To get some fresh air I climbed out the window onto the fire escape.

I was sitting out there one evening when Dmitri and Leah came by together. I heard them talking to Mama inside our apartment. I wondered if Mama knew that, like Dmitri, Leah was also a member of the union.

Anya was on her way to join the union. If enough girls had joined the union they might all be alive today because the Triangle would have closed at noon on that awful day.

Dmitri and Leah climbed through the window to join me on the fire escape. Leah kissed me on both cheeks, then asked, "How are you, Galena? I am so sorry about Anya. She was a dear friend and a wonderful person."

I nodded in agreement. "I'm all right. As well as could be expected, I guess."

Dmitri touched my arm. "Leah and I wanted to come by to tell you something."

Tell me something? What could either of you possibly have to tell me that would be of any importance at all right now? My sister is dead. That is all that is important.

"What is it?" I asked, trying to be as polite as possible, even though I certainly did not feel like being polite to anyone right now, much less Leah. I still could not forgive her for introducing Anya to Dmitri. He had come between my sister and me and had changed our final days together.

Leah leaned in closer and whispered. "As I'm sure you know, there have been protests about the fire all across the city the past few days. People are outraged that something so horrible could have happened, and they are determined that a tragedy like this will never happen again."

I was not sure why Leah was telling me this. What would she expect me to do? I could not leave the apartment during shivah.

"So?" I asked her.

"So we need your help, too, Galena. You must join the protests and give your support. Your sister would have wanted it that way. She was almost ready to join the union. She knew workers, including herself, were being treated unfairly. And now, it's more apparent than ever that workers must stand together to change things for the better."

I could not disagree with anything she was saying. But I could not break shivah. And, besides, what difference could one small girl like me make?

"I cannot leave the apartment now, Leah. You know that," I told her.

Leah glared at me. "Yours is not the only Jewish family to have suffered a tragic loss from this fire. Other Jews are breaking shivah to join the protests. You have mourned your sister for several days. Now honor her by joining our cause."

I glanced at Dmitri. He nodded. "She's right, Galena. Anya would want you to join the protests. Don't worry. You will be safe. I will watch over you."

Suddenly I was fighting mad. I realized how Mama felt when Anya and I suggested she trade her lifelong customs and traditions for the new American ways.

"How do you know what Anya would want, Dmitri? Perhaps you did not know her as well as you think you did. She was my sister. I have known her all my life. She obeyed Mama and followed the traditions and customs that Mama holds dear. Anya would not expect me to cause Mama even more pain right now by refusing to sit shivah!"

I stood, ready to go back into the apartment so I would not have to listen to any more from Leah or Dmitri.

Leah grabbed my arm. "Listen . . . I know what I am about to say will sound terribly cruel, and I don't mean it to be. But you must think about this. In a way, your mama's Old World ways allowed your sister to be killed. There are too many people who still think like your mother. Until everyone is willing to stand up and fight for what is right, things will not change. Do you want to see more girls like your sister die needlessly?"

I jerked free from Leah. "Get away from me!" I said.

Tears rolled down my cheeks as I climbed through the window and returned to our apartment.

Mama did not cause Anya to die. How can you even suggest such a thing, Leah?

I ran to my bed, fell down on it, and sobbed. I was so confused. One minute I felt Leah and Dmitri were kind and caring, the next minute I hated both of them.

How can Dmitri listen to that awful girl? Was I right about him after all? Does he care about the union more than he cared about Anya and more than he cares about Mama now?

Mama and Papa's visitors must have thought I was crying about Anya. One couple leaned down to me on the mattress. A few people patted my back, others offered a few kind words, then quietly told Mama and Papa they would leave us so we could rest. When the apartment was empty of visitors, Mama lay down beside me and rubbed my back.

"My shaineh meydl," she said in Yiddish, then switched to English. "Why do you cry so? Are you still crying for your sister?"

I could not seem to stop crying, but I was not crying for Anya now.

I was crying for Mama.

All her life Mama had tried to be a good person and protect those she loved. But, so many years ago, she had not been able to protect her own sister. She had witnessed her sister's death and would never forgive herself for it,

even though it was not really her fault. And now . . . how could anyone think that Mama had allowed Anya's death to happen? That was so terribly cruel! And so unfair. Mama could not be blamed simply because she clung to her Old World ways. If anyone in our family was to blame for Anya's death, it was me. I was the one who had left her in that burning building!

I sat up and hugged Mama.

"I love you so much, Mama," I said.

She hugged me back. "And I love you, my beautiful girl. Did Dmitri and Leah say things to upset you when they were here?" she asked in her broken English.

She handed me a handkerchief, and I wiped my tears and blew my nose.

"I don't think they meant to be unkind," I said honestly. "But they want me to join the marches to protest the fire."

Mama gently smoothed my hair back from my forehead, then she said, "No, no protest marches. I will not have my one and only remaining daughter be trampled in a mass of angry protesters or be carted off to jail. The fire is over, and nothing anyone can do will bring back Anya or any of the other workers who died that day."

"I know that, Mama. But I am confused. How will things ever change and get better if people here do not protest? I will go right back to work at the Triangle factory,

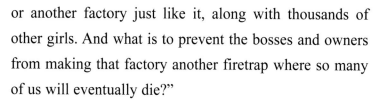

or another factory just like it, along with thousands of other girls. And what is to prevent the bosses and owners from making that factory another firetrap where so many of us will eventually die?"

Mama got that faraway look, the one she always got when she was remembering her own sister.

"I have thought about that very thing," she said, which surprised me. "You will not return to the Triangle Shirtwaist Company . . . or to any other factory for that matter. You will go to school."

"School?" I could not believe what I was hearing. "But we cannot afford for me to go to school, Mama. You know that. We need the salary I earn."

Mama shook her head. "No, we will get by. The remainder of the money I saved to pay the shadchen will now be used to replace your salary. That will get us through for a while. After that, we can always take in boarders as other families here do."

"But, Mama, you have been so proud that we have not had to take in boarders," I protested.

"Quiet," Mama said. "That was just my own foolish notion. Now we will simply have to do what we have to do."

Dmitri returned to our apartment later that evening. This time he was alone. I was glad that Leah was not with

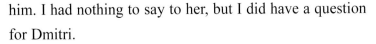

him. I had nothing to say to her, but I did have a question for Dmitri.

"I am sorry for my behavior, earlier, Galena. Leah and I had no right to speak to you that way," he said.

I stared at him blankly and did not answer.

"She certainly should not have blamed your mother for allowing Anya's death. That was unfair and cruel."

I folded my arms across my chest but still did not speak.

"But Leah means well. She really does. She does not mean to accuse and offend the people she cares for, but sometimes she cannot help herself. She thinks it is the only way she can make her point."

I glared at Dmitri. "Well, she made her point all right."

"Will you forgive me, Galena, for allowing Leah to attack you and your mother that way? I am truly sorry."

I did not say anything, and I would not look at him. But I could tell he was genuinely sorry.

Perhaps Dmitri was not unkind and manipulating like Leah.

"I will forgive you," I told him. "Just don't expect me to leave the apartment during shivah and join the protests. I will not upset Mama that way."

Dmitri sat down beside me. "Agreed," he said.

The two of us sat there in silence for a while. Finally, I decided to ask my question.

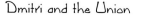

"What was in your pocket the other night, Dmitri?"

He looked puzzled. "What do you mean? I told you. I had a pencil in my pocket."

"Yes, you said that. But it wasn't a pencil I felt when I was using your jacket for a pillow."

He raised his eyebrows, then he said, "Oh . . . I see."

"Well . . . ?" I waited.

"All right, I will tell you. But you must promise not to tell anyone else, particularly your mother. No sense upsetting her now," he said.

"Was it a ring?" I asked.

He nodded. "Yes, an engagement ring. Did you guess?"

"I thought so," I said. "Was it on Anya's finger when she died? I don't remember ever seeing it, and I know I would not have overlooked it."

"No, no. She never wore it on her finger. She wore it around her neck, on the chain with the locket, so no one would see it, yet it would be next to her heart. They gave the ring to me at the morgue the other night, along with the locket. But I took off the ring before I gave you the locket."

I thought back to my last morning with Anya, when we left the apartment for work and I had asked to see the locket, as I always did.

So that's why Anya would not allow me to see the photos inside the locket. I would have seen the ring on the chain, and I would have known the secret she shared with Dmitri.

So many things made sense now. I should have known that Anya would never have parted with her precious locket.

"Is that the secret you and Anya were always whispering and laughing about?"

"Yes," said Dmitri. "We did not mean to hurt you or exclude you from our plans, Galena. You meant the world to Anya, and she hated keeping our secret from you. But Anya said she needed time for your mother to get to know and accept me before we let it be known we were serious about each other. Until then, we could tell no one. Not even you, for fear of hurting your mother."

So I had been wrong about Dmitri in the beginning. He wasn't just a bossy, domineering man. In fact, quite the opposite. He was doing what Anya wanted him to do by keeping their engagement a secret.

I smiled at him. "You really loved Anya, didn't you?"

"With all my heart," he said, choking back tears. "I would have done anything for her. Anything at all. If only I could have saved her . . . "

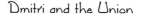

I touched his hand. "And she would have done anything for you. Even defied Mama and married you, if she had to."

"Well, I had hoped it would not come to that," said Dmitri. "Anya and I were both hoping your mother would begin to like and accept me."

I did not want to let Dmitri know that Mama had hired a shadchen who had already found a possible match for Anya. It would be cruel to tell him that now if Anya had not already told him about it. And since he did not mention it, I assumed she had not told him. She was probably planning to tell Mama about the engagement before the meeting with the man the shadchen hoped would be Anya's perfect match. I decided to change the subject.

"Have you been taking part in the protests?" I asked.

"Of course," he said. "I feel that Anya would have wanted me to. She did strongly believe in the union. She was planning on joining as soon as she could convince your mother that it was safe for her to do so."

"And do you really think Anya would have wanted me to join the protests, too?"

"Yes," he said. "I think she would have wanted all of us to march in protest against the fire and the tragic deaths of so many. The fire should never have happened, and something so tragic should certainly never happen again."

"Then tell me about the protests," I said.

Maybe Anya had been right all along, and Mama will have to change her Old World ways about many things, not just matchmakers.

"I'll do more than that," he said, pulling a newspaper out from underneath his jacket. "Look at this!"

Dmitri had circled something in the trade papers in bright red ink.

"NOTICE: THE TRIANGLE SHIRTWAIST CO. beg to notify their customers that they are in good working order. HEADQUARTERS now at 9–11 University Place."

My mouth opened in disbelief. I stared at Dmitri. "How can this be? Why didn't they send me notice and tell me to return to work?" I looked at the date of the paper. Mr. Harris and Mr. Blanck reopened for business just three days after the fire.

"You know why they did not send you notice," said Dmitri. "For every girl who did not return after the fire, there are a dozen more who want to take her place. And not much else has changed either. The day after they opened, the Building Department of New York discovered that 9–11 University Place is not fireproof. Not only that, Mr. Harris and Mr. Blanck had already blocked the exit to the one fire escape with two rows of sewing machines."

I gasped. "No . . . they wouldn't . . . "

"So you see? You see why it is more important than ever that we have a strong union? You must join the protests, Galena."

I wrapped my fingers around the locket hanging from my neck.

What would you want me to do, Anya? What is the right thing to do? Should I disobey Mama again if it is for a good cause?

chapter ten

I Pick Up Anya's Cause

After Dmitri's visit, I started checking the newspaper every day for news about the union and protests about the fire, although I was not always able to get the trade papers. The newsboy who stood outside our apartment each morning let me look at the morning paper without buying it—if I made sure I kept it neat so he could still sell it when I was finished. I could not read the entire paper anyway. My English was not that good. I scanned the headlines, looking for anything about the Triangle Shirtwaist Company fire or the unions.

On Saturday, I noticed a headline that looked important. The newsboy read the article to me. It said a rich society woman named Anne Morgan had rented out the Metropolitan Opera House on behalf of the Women's Trade Union League for the evening of Sunday, April 2. According to the paper, Morgan wanted to have an open meeting to bring people together toward a common goal of reform. Whatever that meant.

When Dmitri came by on Sunday around noon, I was sitting outside on the fire escape. I asked him about the meeting that would take place later that night. "What is reform? What does that word mean?"

"Well, for one thing it means they want to change the current safety and fire regulations for factories and other buildings in the city," he explained.

How could Mama disagree with that?

"So, what will they do at the meeting?"

Dmitri seemed eager to explain. "They will have speakers who present the problems and suggest ways to solve them. Go with me to the meeting, Galena, and you will find out for yourself."

"Why do girls like me need to go to this meeting? There is nothing I can say or do that would help solve such problems."

"Yes, there is," said Dmitri. "Just by being there you will show your support. If every girl who works in a factory shows up, imagine how many people will be there. People will *have* to change the rules and regulations when they see that thousands of workers are concerned about these things."

I supposed he was right. Plus, I did not see how it could be dangerous to simply attend a meeting such as this one. The police would not be dragging girls off to jail for listening to speakers. And, if I went with Dmitri, he would make certain that no one harmed me. I was sure of that. I trusted him now.

Still, I knew there was no way Mama would agree to let me take part in this. Shivah would end today. We would not need to remain at home the entire day. Yet, according to tradition, after shivah we were supposed to go out in public again for the first time as a family. I seriously doubted that Mama and Papa would want to go to union meeting after just finishing mourning for their daughter. I also knew that Mama might still see this meeting as dangerous because thousands of people would probably be there. Mama's nervousness and uneasiness about crowds had not died with Anya. If anything, Mama was probably more fearful of crowds now than ever.

"Do you want me to talk to your mother about the meeting?" asked Dmitri. "Perhaps she would understand better if I explained it to her."

I stood up. "No, I'd better do it," I said. "But you should leave now and let me talk to her."

"All right," said Dmitri. "I will let you convince her yourself. I'll be waiting for you downstairs tonight and we'll go to the meeting together. If you are not there when I arrive, then I will know you were not able to convince her so I will go to the meeting alone."

"Will Leah be with you when you come by tonight?" I frowned.

Dmitri chuckled. "No, she will go with her fiancé, not me."

My mouth opened but no words came out.

"What's the matter?" asked Dmitri. "Why do you look so shocked?"

"Leah has a fiancé? You mean the shadchen was able to find a match for someone like her?"

Dmitri laughed again. "Yes, she has a fiancé, but the shadchen had nothing to do with it. Leah found the perfect match herself."

I was dumbfounded. But when I thought about it, I realized that, of course, Leah would make her own match.

"Well, good for her. I'm glad she has a fiancé. I'm also glad she won't be with you tonight. She's too bossy. I like to do things differently than she wants sometimes, yet she doesn't like to take no for an answer if I disagree with her. You'd better go now, Dmitri, so I can talk to Mama."

I was secretly hoping that Leah had found a match who was as horrible as she was. She did not deserve anyone as kind as Dmitri.

I do like Dmitri, I suppose. I have not wanted to like him, but I do because he is a kind and gentle man.

I went back inside the apartment and Dmitri left.

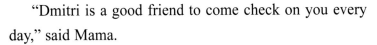

"Dmitri is a good friend to come check on you every day," said Mama.

I was surprised to hear that kind of talk from her. Maybe she was changing her opinion of Dmitri, starting to like him a little more, so it would be easier to talk her into letting me go to the meeting with him tonight.

"Yes, he is a good friend, Mama. He was a good friend to Anya, too. He cared for her very much."

I waited to see how Mama would react to that statement.

Does she have any idea that Anya and Dmitri were in love and planned to be married?

Mama's face softened. "Yes, I may have misjudged him. I thought he was too pushy and only wanted to be Anya's friend to pull one more worker into the union. But I think I was wrong about that."

"Well, did Dmitri say anything to you today when he was here?" I asked.

"Not really," said Mama. "Why? Is there something I need to know?"

I was beginning to lose my nerve.

She'll never agree to let me attend this meeting tonight. What was I thinking? But I must ask.

"Well, he told me about a meeting that will be held at the Metropolitan Opera House tonight. It is an important meeting, Mama. It will help create changes in the safety rules and regulations for factories like the Triangle Shirtwaist Company."

Mama folded her arms across her chest. Not a good sign. She raised her eyebrows. "Good. He can tell you all about this meeting tomorrow," she said.

I took a deep breath.

"He wants me to attend the meeting with him, Mama," I said as quickly as I could get the words out.

"Nonsense," said Mama. "Another of his foolish notions. You will not go out alone after dark with a young man. And you will certainly not attend a meeting with thousands of angry people. It could be quite dangerous, so I don't want to hear anything more about it."

I took another deep breath. There was no sense arguing with Mama.

"Of course not," I said.

Soon after, Mama, Papa, and I went out in public together for the first time since Anya's funeral. Mama had not talked to me about the meeting anymore since earily in the day. We took a simple trip to the market together where Mama and Papa chatted with the shopkeepers they knew, while I enjoyed the sights and smells of all the delicious-looking food. Mama bought eggs, potatoes, and a huge head of cabbage. On the way home, when we came to a pushcart with fresh bread, Mama gave the man pushing the cart two pennies and he handed me a sweet roll. It smelled of cinnamon, and I enjoyed every bite of it right there on the street.

But despite this pleasant experience, I could not stop thinking about the meeting the rest of the afternoon. I opened the locket and stared at the photos inside.

What would you do, Anya? What should I do? I'm the only daughter Mama has left now. I just can't keep disobeying her and lying to her. Yet, somehow I must do what I think is right.

I kept thinking about the owners of the Triangle Shirtwaist Company reopening for business so soon after the fire. The fact that they were still putting girls in danger by blocking the fire exits made me sick to my stomach. By late afternoon, I had made up my mind. I was going to the meeting, whether Mama liked it or not. Selfish men like Mr. Harris and Mr. Blanck should not be allowed to simply move their business to another location and continue to put their workers at risk.

I would be downstairs when Dmitri arrived for me. It would not be very difficult to get away from our apartment before Mama or Papa realized I was gone. I would simply go to the fire escape for fresh air, as I often did. But then I would slip over the fire escape and climb down to the street below.

As it turned out, Mama was resting when the time came to meet Dmitri, and Papa was out on the fire escape, so I eased open the door to the hallway and tiptoed down the stairs. When I pushed open the door to the sidewalk, Dmitri was just walking up to the building.

"Galena, good evening," he said, looking surprised. "So you convinced your mother to let you go, huh? How did you do it?"

I could not risk Mama or Papa realizing I was gone, even before I got away from our apartment building. Papa would demand that I come back into the apartment, and I would not have the nerve to disobey him if he stood before me.

I grabbed Dmitri's hand and pulled him along, "I'll tell you later. Let's get going now so we won't be late."

The Metropolitan Opera House was located in the garment district at 1423 Broadway. It occupied the whole block between West Thirty-ninth Street and West Fortieth Street on the west side of the street, making it hard to miss. I knew where it was and so did Dmitri.

By the time we got there, thousands of people of many different backgrounds and occupations were crowding into the opera house. But most of them were working girls and other East Side immigrants, just like me. They seemed as excited as I was to be there, but I had to remind myself that this was not meant to be a time of enjoyable entertainment. This was a serious meeting. Still, that did not keep me from being thrilled at the beautifully decorated opera house and all the important people who arrived in fancy carriages. As we stood outside in the crowd, watching these people arrive, I could tell that some of the women were very, very wealthy, just by the way they were dressed.

"Why do such wealthy woman care about the garment workers?" I asked Dmitri. "These women have probably never worked a day in their lives, and I'm sure they will never have to."

"Yes, you're right about that," he told me. "They don't need to work for a living. Yet, they think all women, rich and poor, will benefit if women get the right to vote. Many of these women helped with the Uprising of the 20,000, so I'm not surprised they are helping the cause now."

I had expected a crowd, but not one this large. We filed into the opera house and up to the balconies. Down in the orchestra seats sat important-looking men and women, the ones who were dressed so well. A group of people who represented many different parts of society (I could tell by the way they were dressed, some seemed wealthy, others were more like me) sat on stage. The hall was packed. Dmitri told me that most of those at the meeting were members of the Women's Trade Union League.

As I scanned the crowd, I reached inside the collar of my dress and pulled out Anya's locket. I opened it and

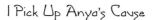

smiled at the picture of Mama, Papa, Anya, and me, and the other photo of Bubbie.

Anya, you would be proud of me for being here tonight. I know you would. Oh, how I wish you could be here, too, Bubbie. I think you would be proud of me, also. And, Mama, someday perhaps you will understand why I am doing this, and you will be proud of me as well.

Dmitri noticed me looking at the photos. "You are so much like your sister," he said, smiling. "She once told me that she opened that locket dozens of times each day to look at her family. She said admiring their photos gave her strength because it helped her realize she was working hard every day to support them, and that made her proud." He brushed away a tear from his cheek, then sat up straight. "Anyway, Anya would be very proud of you tonight, too."

I looked at Anya's face smiling up at me from the photo, then I closed the locket and tucked it back inside my clothes, where it would be safe. "I know she would be proud," I said. "And I feel she is with us tonight, Dmitri. Anya is here watching over all of us."

Dmitri squeezed my hand as one of the distinguished-looking ladies on stage got up and opened the meeting. Then one by one, the other people assembled there stood up to speak. Dmitri told me they were a panel and included many community, church, charity, and government leaders. Each time one of them would start to speak, the crowd offered loud cheers of support or hisses of anger, and I could not hear anything the speaker was saying. Some of the speakers stopped when that happened and waited for the crowd to get quiet before they would continue.

When a young woman about Anya's age, named Rose Schneiderman, got up to speak, the crowd roared and I could not hear a thing she said for a while.

"Who is she?" I asked Dmitri. "Why are they cheering her? She is so young. She can't be any older than Anya."

Dmitri leaned closer so I could hear him. "She is a leader of the Shirtwaist Makers Union and one of those who led the strike at Triangle two years ago. Listen closely to what she has to say, Galena."

The crowd was still and silent as Rose spoke softly but determinedly. She told the crowd, "I would be a traitor to those poor burned bodies, if I were to come here to talk good fellowship. We have tried you good people of the public—and we have found you wanting. . . . This is not the first time girls have been burned alive in this city."

Rose went on to say there were so many workers for one job that it did not seem to matter if 140 or so were burned to death. The crowd roared with anger and support at that, and I felt as angry as everyone else did.

It should matter greatly if even a single person is killed in a needless fire. It should matter greatly if even a single girl lies dead in the street.

I cheered for Rose with the rest of the crowd before I even knew what I was doing. Dmitri looked at me and smiled.

For the first time, I realized why Anya loved Dmitri so much, and I knew how she felt when he showed up every evening at the Asch building, ready to walk us home. She had been right. He was not bossy or a silly flatterer. He cared for Anya and wanted to protect her.

It would have been wrong for Anya to marry anyone but Dmitri. Mama did not need to hire a shadchen. Anya had found her perfect match.

By the time the meeting was over, I felt strong and hopeful that things would be done to improve the safety and working conditions for all of us in the factories.

But what will Mama do when she finds out I have attended this meeting? And how will she react when I tell her I intend on one day joining the Garment Worker's Union?

I did not know the answers to those questions, but I knew it was time to go home to find out.

On the walk home, Dmitri asked me what I thought of the meeting. "Were you afraid?" he asked. "Afraid of all the people there."

I smiled at him and twirled around on the sidewalk. "Afraid? Why, heavens no! It was exciting to see so many people gathered there for a common cause. It made me feel strong."

"Good," said Dmitri. "I'm glad you feel that way. Together, we *can* be strong—strong enough to make a difference. We can make sure that all workers in this city are protected."

Dmitri held open the door to our apartment building for me when we got there, but I did not go in.

"You don't need to walk me to my door," I told him. Since he did not know that Mama had not given me permission to attend the meeting, I did not want him to find out. Besides that, Mama was sure to be very angry with me, and Dmitri did not need to see that either. Plus, she would be just as angry with him if she knew I went to the meeting with him. She would think he was filling my head with foolish notions just as she thought he had done with Anya.

"It's no trouble, Galena," he said. "As a gentleman, I need to know you make it safely to your front door."

I could tell there was no use arguing about it. I entered the building and flew up the stairs ahead of him.

"Okay, I'm home. Thank you, Dmitri, and good night."

I flung open the door to our apartment and nearly jumped into the room before slamming the door shut behind me.

Mama and Papa were alone in the apartment sitting at the table. Papa was reading something, and Mama was darning a sock. They both looked up, but neither of them said anything at first. Mama glared at me. "Where have you been?" she demanded finally.

I froze. I did not know what to say or do.

"We were worried about you, Galena," said Papa. "Where have you been by yourself after dark? How can you worry us so, right after the death of your sister?"

Papa was right, of course. It had been selfish of me to make them worry.

I stood up straight. "I was at the meeting at the Metropolitan Opera House," I told them. "The meeting I told you about, Mama."

Mama set the sock she was darning on the table. She stood in front of me. "The meeting I forbid you to attend, you mean."

I nodded and looked at the floor. My confidence drained away suddenly. I could not meet Mama's eyes.

"I'm sorry, Mama, but I had to go. It was a way to honor Anya."

I waited for her to scream at me or punish me in some way. But she did neither of those things.

"You honor your sister by disobeying your mother? I don't think so. Now go to bed. We will talk about this in the morning."

"But, Mama . . ."

"Hush!" she said. "I told you to go to bed."

"Do as your mother says, Galena," said Papa.

I pulled the curtain across the room to give myself a little privacy to change clothes and go to sleep without Mama and Papa glaring at me. I removed my shoes, changed into my nightgown, and climbed into bed, where I pulled the covers up under my chin. I wished Mama could have been at the meeting with me, to feel the strength of the crowd and the powerful feeling that I had absorbed from them. Maybe then she would have changed her mind about the union as I had done.

I reached for the locket inside my nightgown. I opened it and stared at Anya's picture.

I am no longer your Little Shadow, Anya. But I can't become Mama's shadow now either. I have to do what I think is right. And after listening to all those people at the meeting tonight, I know that supporting the union is the right thing to do.

Early the next morning, Mama took me to the market again, to buy something she had forgotten the day before. As we made our way through the crowds, I was hoping we would not run into Dmitri. But I was sure he would be at work, so I did not worry about it very much. Many workers had refused to return to their jobs since the fire. But most of the union workers had gone back to theirs. Dmitri had no idea how angry Mama was that I had gone to the meeting at the Metropolitan Opera House. Of course, he had no idea that Mama had forbidden me to go and I had disobeyed her and sneaked out of the apartment to join him last night. I didn't want him to find out either. And I certainly did not want Mama to blame Dmitri for what I had done.

Once Mama and I were home from shopping, she and Papa said they wanted to speak with me.

Oh, no . . . here it comes! My punishment for going to the meeting last night.

"Sit down with us at the table," said Papa. He pulled out a chair for me and one for himself. Mama was busy making tea. She put the teapot and three teacups on the table, then she poured a cup of tea for Papa and set it in front of him.

"I don't care for any tea, Mama," I said.

"All right." She poured a cup for herself while I waited.

Finally, Papa spoke.

"Since shivah ended yesterday, I will begin searching for new work."

I stared at him.

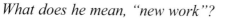

What does he mean, "new work"?

"Won't you just return to your old job?" I asked him.

"Do you think they would take me back after missing work so many days to sit shivah? Ha!" he said. "What do they care if we have been in mourning? They have orders to fill. That is all that matters to them. No, I must find a new job tomorrow, and I will."

He took a sip of tea.

"Then I shall look for a new job, too," I told him.

Mama set down her teacup.

"No," she said. "You will go to school."

"But, Mama," I protested, "I don't want to go to school."

Papa looked at me.

"Your mother and I have discussed this. You will go to school. You will be safe there. In a few years, when you have finished school, you can return to work, but not until then."

I clenched my fists. I felt my face redden.

"You'll do anything to keep me from ever joining the union. Won't you, Mama?" I blurted out. "I don't want to quit my job. I love working with all the other girls. I don't want to go to school."

Mama looked at me sternly. "We have finished talking," she said. "It is settled. You will go to school."

That evening around five thirty, I sat on the front stoop to our building. I was certain Dmitri would come by on his way home from work, and he did. He had something to tell me.

"Have you heard about the mass funeral and march that will take place on Wednesday?" he asked.

I nodded. "They'll march to Evergreen Cemetery to bury the bodies no one was able to identify. Isn't that right?"

"Yes," said Dmitri. "It is a mass funeral, but it will be more than that. It will be a chance for people across the city to show their support for the common laborers. It should be the biggest procession this city has ever seen."

I could hardly imagine such a thing.

"Will you join me, Galena?" he asked. "I will come by for you, and we will march in the procession together. Perhaps your mother and father will want to join us."

What could I say?

I could not very well tell him that Mama and Papa were angry with me for going to the meeting with him the other evening.

Or could I?

"Dmitri," I said. "I need to tell you something. Sit here on the stoop with me."

Dmitri sat down beside me. "What is it? Is something wrong?"

I stared at the street. I could not look him in the eye.

"Mama and Papa say I cannot return to work. They say I must go to school instead."

Surprisingly, Dmitri smiled. "That is good news, Galena. I am happy for you."

I looked up at him and frowned.

"That is not good news at all, Dmitri! Without my salary, we will have to take in boarders. Mama has never wanted that."

Dmitri leaned back so his elbows rested on the steps behind him.

"What your mother really wants is your safety, Galena. Before the fire, she thought you were safe at work. If she had known that wasn't the case, I'm sure she would have taken in boarders and sent you to school the moment you arrived in this country," he said.

"But what about the union?" I asked. "If I go back to school I won't be able to do anything important that will help workers like Anya and the others who died."

Dmitri sat up straight and touched my hand.

"Yes, you will. With an education you can help workers everywhere, not just the garment workers here in New York."

I hugged my knees and rocked back and forth.

"But I want to do something helpful now, not years from now when I am older."

Dmitri chuckled. "Okay, then. Join the march on Wednesday. I will come get you and we can go together."

I studied the sidewalk in front of me.

"Well, let me think about it," I said finally.

Dmitri stood up. "What's to think about?"

Mama and Papa, that's what.

But I didn't say that.

Dmitri told me he would come by my family's apartment again on Wednesday and wait outside for a few minutes. If I did not come downstairs, he would know I had decided not to attend the funeral and the march.

This time I did not say a word about the mass funeral and the march to Mama. What good would it have done? She would never have agreed to let me go.

chapter eleven

A New Life
for My Family

Wednesday, April 5, 1911, was a gray, rainy day. Low-hanging clouds and fog hid the tops of buildings. The weather seemed most appropriate for what was to take place that day. It was as if the heavens knew the International Ladies' Garment Workers' Union had declared this an official day of mourning. A mass funeral for the unknown victims of the fire and a march to honor them would take place. All stores and businesses in the city would be closed today.

Mama and Papa knew about the plans for the funeral and the march, even though I hadn't mentioned anything to them. Still, Mama must have realized that I would want to go.

"With thousands of people upset about those lost in the fire, the crowd might get hysterical and violent. It sounds too dangerous, Galena," Mama said, showing me an article in the newspaper announcing the mass funeral. "We will not join the march. Not Papa, not me, and certainly not you. So I do not want to hear anything about it."

Why are you always so afraid of everything, Mama? Why are you so afraid to take a stand?

"Fine," I told her, trying to appear totally uninterested in the march.

A little while later, I sat in the ground floor doorway of our apartment building with a group of younger children who lived on the floor above us. The door was propped open and we watched huge raindrops bounce off the sidewalk. Puddles had started to form.

Do I dare meet Dmitri for the funeral procession? If I do, will Mama disown me when she finds out where I have gone? Do I dare worry her and Papa again so soon after Anya's death?

I fingered Anya's locket. This time, I did not need to open it and see Anya's photo to gain strength. Mama's own words came back to me now: *Your life experiences make you who you are forever, Galena.*

The experience of losing my sister would not make me quiet and afraid, like Mama had become when her own sister was killed. I was determined it would make me strong and ready to stand up for myself and for others.

The rain slackened off for a few minutes.

There was no more time left for thinking.

I must act.

But before I could move, I felt a hand on my shoulder. I gulped. "Papa . . . "

"Do not be afraid, Galena," said Papa. "I know you have been trying to decide if you should defy your mother again and meet Dmitri for the funeral procession."

I turned to face him. "You do?"

"Of course I do," said Papa. "You want to honor your sister and your friends who died with her."

"Papa," I said, then I reached out to hug him. "Is that so wrong? Why can't Mama understand?"

"Because she is afraid, in her own way," said Papa. "And, no. It is not wrong to honor your sister." Papa handed me an umbrella. "Take this. Go meet Dmitri. I will talk to Mama. I will make her understand about the union."

I pulled away from Papa and took the umbrella. "You will?"

"I will," said Papa. "Now go."

He kissed the top of my head.

I dashed out the door, opened the umbrella, and took off down the sidewalk, eager to meet Dmitri. By the time I got to the corner, he had just turned onto Orchard Street. He had his own umbrella.

"Dmitri!" I called out.

He smiled as I approached him.

Together, we walked quickly under our umbrellas. The rain was falling harder again now.

Will anyone even come to the funeral procession in weather like this?

We had walked only a short distance when I noticed them—lines of people standing on the sidewalks under black umbrellas.

There were so many of them huddled together, they looked like rows of big black mushrooms.

Dmitri and I fell into one of the lines.

Soon the lines started to move, everyone walking silently.

There were ladies in fancy lamb's wool coats.

Surely these ladies are accustomed to riding in automobiles, not walking through the streets in the rain, being splashed by passing vehicles.

Yet, today, they walked with the rest of us.

The crowd grew and grew at each turn. Soon we were near Washington Square, and women in the crowd began to whimper as we came closer to Washington Place and Greene Street, closer to the scene of the fire. They cried softly at first, then thousands of voices mingled to produce a sound of thunderous grief.

It was like nothing I had ever heard before.

And like nothing I hoped to ever hear again.

We kept marching. After awhile, the crowd grew silent again.

At Fifth Avenue, we met another army of marchers, as large as our own. There were hundreds of thousands of us marching now. We passed buildings as tall and as unsafe as the Asch building. People were leaning out the windows, watching us as we passed by.

Here and there, an older woman would coax a young girl to join her under the safety of her umbrella or inside her warm coat.

To see people taking care of one another like that was a beautiful sight among all the sadness.

When we got to the entrance of Evergreen Cemetery, hundreds were there, waiting in the heavy rain. They were silent, too.

Men stood holding their hats in their hands. Tears, mingled with raindrops, streamed down people's cheeks. Yet noisy children raced through the grounds, jumping over and on the graves, reminding everyone that life goes on, no matter what horrible things happen.

Eight coffins were resting alongside a large pit that had recently been dug. It was muddy, and a small tent stood at the end of it. A few city officials stood in front of the tent huddled under umbrellas.

Since I had heard from friends whenever there was news related to the fire, I knew that only seven bodies had remained unidentified. For that reason, I could not understand why there were eight coffins until one of the officials explained that the eighth coffin "contains the dismembered fragments picked up at the fire by the police."

I shivered, imagining what was inside that eighth coffin.

One by one, the officials spoke.

Rabbi Judah L. Magnus was the last to come forward and speak. When the rabbi finished speaking, I turned to Dmitri.

"The people in this city must learn to change their ways," I said to him. "You know that, and Anya knew that. Now I think Papa knows it, too."

I wrapped the fingers of my free hand around Anya's gold locket.

I think Papa will join the union, Anya. And I will help our family by going to school. One day I will join the union, too.

Slowly the crowd moved out of the cemetery. I knew that it would be a long time before the victims' families, and the entire city of New York, recovered from the tragic fire at the Triangle Shirtwaist Company. So, as we marched toward home, I still felt sad.

But now, for the first time since Anya's death, I also felt hopeful.

the end

This 1907 photo of the sewing room of a clothing factory in Troy, New York, shows the cramped conditions that workers at the Triangle Shirtwaist Company experienced.

The Real History Behind the Story

From 1824 to 1924, 34 million immigrants came to America from Europe. Many of these people were trying to escape starvation, religious persecution, or unfair or changing governments. Millions of these immigrants settled in New York City, where the majority of them had entered the country. Most of them were poor and knew little about American life, just like Galena and her family. They soon found that the cost of living in their new country was much more expensive than it had been in their homelands. For that reason, many families had to take in boarders to help pay their rent and other expenses.

Unsafe Factories

Children often worked alongside adults in unsafe factories such as the Triangle Shirtwaist Company. Such places were called sweatshops, and they had one thing in common: They were all places where men, women, and children worked under the worst conditions. Sweatshops were usually hot in the summer and cold in the winter and had poor ventilation and little lighting. Cotton fibers drifted throughout the rooms, and the air was often filled with fumes from charcoal heaters or gasoline stoves.

The Fire

On Saturday, March 25, 1911, a fire broke out at the Triangle Shirtwaist Company just as workers were leaving for the day. No one ever found out what caused the fire,

A horse-drawn fire engine races to the scene of the Triangle Shirtwaist Company fire on March 25, 1911, in New York City.

although some people thought it started when the motor that supplied power for the two hundred sewing and cutting machines on the eighth floor emitted a flame that set fire to fabric cuttings nearby.

Triangle workers were mostly young immigrant girls like Galena and Anya. Many of them spoke little or no English and some worked for mere pennies a day. An entire week's wages for many workers might be less than five dollars, which explains why Galena was so proud of herself for earning twelve dollars for two weeks pay.

The Triangle fire spread rapidly throughout the eighth, ninth, and tenth floors of the Asch building, which ironically was considered fireproof. The fire lasted less than thirty minutes. Yet, by the time it was over, it had claimed the lives of 146 people. All but 21 of these were females, mostly around fourteen years old. After the fire, a total of eleven engagement rings were found among the dead young women.

Unsafe working conditions caused most of the deaths from the fire. The factory owners locked the doors from the outside so the girls could not leave the building without first having their pocketbooks checked to be sure they were not trying to steal pieces of fabric or spools of thread. Isaac Harris and Max Blanck, the owners of the Triangle Shirtwaist Company, also wanted the doors locked so union representatives could not enter the building and try to talk to the workers about joining the union. In addition, the fire escapes were so flimsy that they collapsed and killed many of the workers who were trying to escape from the building that day.

The Trial

After the fire, Harris and Blanck were indicted for manslaughter in April 1911, and they went to trial on December 4, 1911. The trial lasted for eighteen days, and more than one hundred fifty witnesses were called to testify about whether the doors to the factory were locked, if the owners knew they were locked, and whether the locked doors led to the death of Margaret Schwartz, one of the workers there. Worker after worker testified that he or she could not open the doors to the only escape route (the stairs to the Washington Place exit). The stairs on the Greene Street side were completely covered by flames. Before the jury left to decide whether Harris and Blanck were guilty, the judge told them that the key to the case was whether Harris and Blanck knew that the door was locked. The jury

154 KILLED IN SKYSCRAPER FACTORY FIRE; SCORES BURN, OTHERS LEAP TO DEATH.

700 WORKERS, MOSTLY GIRLS, TRAPPED;

The New York *World* reported on the fire on March 26, 1911, the day after the tragedy. At the time, reporters thought more people had been killed than actually had been.

deliberated less than two hours before returning with a verdict of not guilty.

Twenty-three civil suits were brought against Harris and Blanck. On March 11, 1913, three years after the fire, the two men settled. They were ordered to pay damages of just seventy-five dollars to each of the twenty-three families who had sued them.

Unions and Reform

Two years before the tragic Triangle Shirtwaist fire, more than twenty thousand garment workers went out on strike against poor working conditions and low pay. The strikers had a simple list of demands, and most shops in New York had met these demands by February 1910, so the union called off the strike. The Triangle Shirtwaist Company was one of the shops that did not agree to the strikers' demands, so the workers at Triangle were no better off after the strike than they were before it.

It took the tragic Triangle fire of 1911 to create any changes in laws that would protect factory workers at all shops. After the tragedy, the legislature established the Factory Investigating Commission. Its job was to study issues related to the health and safety of workers, the condition of the buildings in which they worked, and

These two women were part of the picket line during the garment workers' strike of 1910, which came to be known as the "Uprising of the 20,000."

additional necessary laws and ordinances. As a result of the findings of this commission, laws were established that started to create safer working environments for factory workers. Investigators regularly visited workplaces to see that the conditions there were safe for workers. More workers than ever joined the unions and the unions became strong bargaining forces for them.

New Challenges

After the mid-1970s, the number of investigators who made sure conditions were safe in America's factories declined due to budget cuts. By 1996, there were so few investigators that they could not possibly keep up with enforcing the laws, so sweatshops began to reappear.

UNITE (formerly the Union of Needletrades, Industrial and Textile Employees) and HERE (Hotel Employees and Restaurant Employees International Union) merged on July 8, 2004, forming UNITE HERE. Today, the union faces many of the same problems that earlier unions did, yet organizing new workers into the union is a top priority, and UNITE-HERE fights for workers everywhere, not only in the United States.